THE TRUE HEART

HELENA HALME

COPYRIGHT

ACKNOWLEDGMENTS

I couldn't have written this novel without the support of my long-suffering husband. The original Englishman is an excellent first reader, but even a better cook. I am also grateful for my editor, Dorothy Stannard, who tirelessly and patiently has worked with me on the many versions of this book. Thanks must also go to my naval expert, Adam Peters, for all his invaluable advice. It goes without saying that all mistakes intentional or not, are entirely down to me, or required for fictional purposes.

PREFACE

Will I spend my life longing for him? Or feeling guilty about a secret I'm keeping from him?

ONE

Kaisa was trying to concentrate on the news bulletin she was preparing for broadcast later that afternoon when the phone on her desk rang.

'Hello, darling!' It was Rose.

Kaisa tried to hide her disappointment. 'How lovely to hear from you,' she said, lifting her voice higher than it normally was. She stifled a sigh in her hand and decided not to think about Peter. He was due home from a long patrol any moment, so when a phone call was put through to her at work, Kaisa immediately thought it must be her husband. He usually called from somewhere in Scotland as soon as he could, to tell her he was safe. Kaisa hadn't spoken to Peter for over six weeks and she was desperate to hear his voice.

'I'm up in town and wondered if I could see you after work?' Rose said, unaware of Kaisa's disappointment.

Rose met Kaisa outside Bush House, the headquarters of the BBC's World Service in Aldwych, central London, where Kaisa had been working for over three years.

'You look good!' Kaisa said, hugging her friend hard.

1

She felt bad for wishing it hadn't been Rose on the phone. She rarely saw her good friend these days, not since she'd retired to the country.

'How's Peter?' Rose asked, letting go of Kaisa.

'On patrol, 'she said, trying not to sound too miserable.

'You poor darling, I don't know how you do it!' Rose suggested they hop into a cab. 'Terroni's, yes?' she said. Kaisa nodded.

Kaisa loved the Italian café where she'd worked a few years ago, even if she had to cross town to visit it. During the months she'd been a waitress there, Kaisa had become one of the family and had even learned some Italian. She'd spent one potentially lonely Christmas Day with the Terroni family, and after that the Farringdon café, with its large steaming coffee machine, small round tables and curved chairs, and the best coffee in London, had been like home to her. Kaisa had got to know Rose, who had introduced her to Toni, the head of the Terroni family, through Duncan, a former friend of Peter's.

Rose had been instrumental in Kaisa's career. She'd first employed Kaisa at the feminist magazine *Adam's Apple,* which she'd run in the mid-eighties, then encouraged her to attend journalism school, and eventually to apply for a job in the BBC's Finnish section. Without Rose, Kaisa was certain she'd still be living in Helsinki, miserable and divorced from Peter, and probably working for a bank like her university friend Tuuli. Not that Tuuli was unhappy, far from it, but work in finance suited her, whereas Kaisa knew it would have made her miserable.

When she'd first met Rose, Duncan's cousin, during a trip to London from Portsmouth, she'd thought her the most glamorous person she'd ever met. Her hair, clothes and manner had reminded Kaisa of Princess Diana.

Kaisa had been newly married and had only lived in the UK for a matter of months, but Rose had offered Kaisa a job as her assistant during a boozy meeting in one of the city's fashionable wine bars.

Peter's career had taken the couple to Scotland, so Kaisa hadn't been able to accept the job in London. Sometimes she wondered what would have happened if she'd refused to move up to Faslane, and had accepted the London job at that point in her life instead of later. At the time, Peter and Kaisa had both thought the idea of living in London impossible; Kaisa's salary wouldn't have covered the living costs, and with Peter serving on a Polaris submarine, going away to sea for weeks on end, they would never have seen each other.

Kaisa grinned as she sat down opposite Rose. It was the life they had now, so why couldn't they have tried it sooner?

'What's so funny?' Rose asked.

'Nothing, just thinking of the past,' Kaisa replied. She gazed at her friend. Rose was quite a few years older than her, and since her move away from London and marriage to Roger, she'd put on a little weight. The added roundness suited her. Her face, framed by dark unruly curls, now mixed with grey, looked softer, and the few lines around her pale eyes just made her look friendlier.

'You look very happy,' Kaisa said and put her hand on Rose's as it rested on the table.

They'd been through the obligatory hugs and kisses from the café owner, Toni, and his wife, and 'Mamma', and were now facing each other at one of the corner tables by the window, their favourite, which Toni – miraculously – was always able to reserve for them.

'No point in dwelling,' Rose said.

'I guess not,' Kaisa said and thought about her own

present condition, which wasn't a condition anymore. She was just about to tell Rose about it, when her friend said quickly, as if to get something out of the way, 'But talking of the past, I saw Duncan last weekend.'

'Oh,' Kaisa said and watched her friend as she lowered her eyes and fiddled with her large diamond engagement ring, now next to a gold wedding band on the ring finger of her left hand. Kaisa knew Rose felt guilty and responsible for the affair between Kaisa and her cousin Duncan. Rose believed that Duncan had used her in order to impress Kaisa, and in a way that was right.

On the very night that Duncan had first introduced Kaisa to Rose, who had scheduled a date for a job interview with her, Duncan had tried to seduce Kaisa in his house in Chelsea. That had been the first time. Kaisa had barricaded herself in the guest bedroom, and the next morning had believed Duncan's profuse apologies and promises never to try anything like that with her ever again.

Yet Kaisa knew she had gone to bed with Duncan willingly months later in Faslane; it was her unhappiness at being so far away from home, frustration at not being able to find a job, and her loneliness without her new husband that had contributed to the events of that awful night.

In a way, Kaisa had also benefited from the guilt Rose had felt; she'd done so much for Kaisa that Kaisa herself often felt bad. They had discussed these feelings many times over the years, often without mentioning Duncan's name. Kaisa didn't want to think back to her awful mistake, and she also understood that Rose had severed all ties to him and didn't want to talk about her cousin. Kaisa was surprised that her friend mentioned Duncan now.

Rose lifted her cup of coffee up to her lips and gazed at Kaisa over the rim. 'He's not very well.'

Kaisa swallowed a mouthful of the strong black coffee and put her cup down.

Rose told her that Duncan had been unwell with a severe flu during the winter. A week ago he'd been to see a specialist and been diagnosed with AIDS. Rose whispered the last word, and looked around the café to see if anyone was listening to their conversation.

'AIDS!' Kaisa exclaimed.

'Shh, keep your voice down,' Rose said and leaned over the table to take hold of Kaisa's hand. 'I'm only telling you so that you go and get tested.'

Kaisa stared at her friend, 'Tested, me?'

'And if you have it, Peter may have it too. And all his – and your – sexual partners for the past five years.'

'Oh, my God,' Kaisa felt her heartbeat quicken. The thought of having to tell Peter he had to go for an HIV test was beyond Kaisa. And for Peter to have to tell the two women he'd had affairs with while she and Peter had been separated would be unthinkable.

'And Ravi?' Kaisa gasped.

Rose nodded.

Kaisa felt sick. She took another sip of her coffee, but it suddenly tasted vile. 'But we're trying for a baby.'

'I know, that's why I wanted to tell you so that you can get tested in case ...'

Kaisa was quiet. Her mind was full of ifs and buts.

'Look, it's highly unlikely you have it. Duncan, as I understand it, has been more active sexually since you two, were, you know, together. I'm sure he was fine before.'

Kaisa sat with her hand over her mouth. She caught sight of Toni, who was watching the two women from his usual post behind the glass counter. Kaisa took her hand away and attempted to smile at him. The café owner

5

nodded and waved a cup in his hand, asking if they needed a fill-up. Kaisa shook her head vigorously; the last person she wanted to tell Rose's news to was Toni. That would mean half of London would know it by supper time.

'But I thought he was living in the country?' Kaisa remembered a letter she'd received from Duncan, and immediately destroyed, when she was staying in Helsinki after the separation from Peter. He'd complained about the lack of female company in the countryside. Suddenly, Kaisa realised. Duncan must be gay! Or bisexual.

Rose raised her eyebrows. 'It only takes one sexual partner to be infected.'

Kaisa nodded. 'Of course,' then added carefully, 'But I thought you could only get it from gay sex?'

'No, that's not true!' Rose said emphatically. 'Anyone can get it.'

'Oh,' Kaisa said. Suddenly a picture she'd seen of a family somewhere in America, where a father was hugging his dying son with AIDS, came to her mind. In the photo the son had sunken cheeks and eyes, and his father's face was twisted in anguish as he embraced his son. And she thought about Freddie Mercury. There had been reports that he had AIDS. He'd looked thin and gaunt in the pictures Kaisa had seen in the papers.

Kaisa's thoughts returned to Duncan.

'How is he?'

Suddenly, Rose burst into tears, and before Kaisa could do or say anything, Toni and Mamma had come over and were making a scene, talking loudly and asking what the matter was.

Kaisa managed to calm her adoptive Italian family down, and eventually after they had made sure 'Rosa', as Toni insisted on calling Rose, was fine, Rose and Kaisa left the café and walked along the Clerkenwell Road towards Holborn. While they waited to cross the busy Grays Inn Road, walking arm in arm, Rose told Kaisa how Duncan had pneumonia, and the doctors were concerned about him. 'He's just not getting better, Kaisa,' Rose said. Her eyes filled with tears again and Kaisa pulled her into The Yorkshire Grey, a large pub on the corner of Theobalds Road.

'I think we need something a bit stronger than coffee,' Kaisa said.

Rose nodded and settled herself into a corner table. The pub was quickly filling up with post-work drinkers, but it wasn't yet crowded. It was a few minutes past five o'clock on a Friday evening after all, Kaisa thought. The sun streamed into the dark space, making the interior feel stuffy.

Rose took a large gulp of her glass of wine and said, 'Look, I know it's unfair of me to say so, but he's been asking after you.'

'What?'

'Actually, he's been talking about both you and Peter.'

Kaisa looked at Rose. Seeing her friend so upset and the news about AIDS were affecting Kaisa's head. The room began to sway in front of her eyes. Suddenly all the memories of the first year of her marriage came into her mind. After the months she and Peter had spent apart, when Kaisa had forged her own career, finally getting the coveted job as a reporter at the World Service, she had tried to forget about Duncan, and her infidelity. When she and Peter had eventually reunited after several false starts and misunderstandings, they had vowed to forgive each other and forget the past. Since then, they had rarely spoken about the events leading up to their separation, or about the other relationships they both had had during that time.

'He needs to see that you've forgiven him.' Rose said,

placing a hand over Kaisa's arm. Her pale blue eyes were pleading with Kaisa.

Kaisa said, with hesitation, 'You can tell him there are no hard feelings.'

Rose tilted her head sideways, and took another large gulp of wine. 'You don't understand.'

It was Kaisa's turn to take hold of Rose's hands, resting on the small, grubby mock teak table. 'What, tell me!'

'He is staying with us, Roger and I, and I wondered, well, we wondered ...' Rose began to dig inside her handbag for a tissue. She blew her nose, soliciting sideways glances from a group of men in pinstripe suits who were drinking pints of beer at the bar. When Rose had recovered a little, she finished her wine and Kaisa said, 'Want another?'

'Yes, let me,' Rose went back to her handbag, but Kaisa replied, 'No this is on me. You've bought enough drinks for me in the past.' She smiled, and got a nod from Rose.

Back at the table, when Kaisa was again facing Rose over their glasses of wine, Rose took a deep breath. 'I wondered if you might be able to come and see him.'

Kaisa stared at her friend. 'I, I don't know ...' she hadn't set eyes on Duncan since the awful fight between him and Peter in the pool. Duncan hadn't even turned up at Peter's Court Martial a few weeks later. He'd been dismissed his ship immediately after the fight, when his actions, 'unbecoming an officer of Her Majesty's Service' against a fellow naval officer, had come to light, and he'd left Faslane by all accounts that same night.

'Please, do this for me. I know his behaviour has been despicable, but he is a dying man.' Now tears were running down Rose's cheeks.

Kaisa glanced at the men behind her, and put her hands over Rose's on the sticky table.

'Of course I'll come,' she heard herself say, even though she had no idea how she would be able to face Duncan. Or how she would tell Peter any of it: her planned visit to see her former lover, or the AIDS tests they may both have to take. Or the consequences for their plans to start a family. *What a mess she had created.*

TWO

When Kaisa heard the phone ring as soon as she stepped inside their terraced house in Notting Hill, she knew that this time it must be Peter. She dropped the bag of cheese, ham and a small loaf of sliced bread that she'd picked up from the corner shop onto the floor and hurried to the phone in the hall.

'Hi darling,' Peter's voice sounded tired.

'How are you?' It was wonderful to hear Peter's voice. She'd not seen him for over two months, and hadn't spoken to him for weeks.

'I'm good. Tired. We've had a royal visit so we've literally just docked. It'll take at least two to three days for the debrief.'

Kaisa sat down on the wooden bench that she and Peter had found in a second-hand shop the week they moved into their new home three years ago. It had one wobbly leg, but there never seemed to be enough time to fix it while Peter was at home. She was silent while she waited for what she knew would be the next thing Peter said. He wouldn't be coming home that evening.

To delay the inevitable, and to hide her disappointment, Kaisa said, 'A royal visit! Who?' She tried to sound enthusiastic. She knew how boring life onboard the submarine could be, and how a VIP could boost the crew's morale, including that of the officers.

'Lady Di.'

'What?'

'Yes, it was a surprise to us too,' Kaisa could hear Peter's grin and saw the handsome face of her husband in her mind. How she missed him!

'She came onboard at the Cumbrae Gap and afterwards insisted on visiting the families at the Drumfork Club.'

'Oh.' The name of the place where Peter had suffered the humiliation of a Court Martial put a stop to Kaisa's questions.

'She was so lovely, just natural, talking to all the wives as if she was one of them. You should've been there!'

Kaisa was taken aback a second time. Peter knew full well why she wasn't living up in Faslane with all the other Navy Wives. They'd tried it and it nearly cost them their marriage. Kaisa took a deep breath and decided she wouldn't let her disappointment show.

'What was she wearing?' she asked instead.

Peter's laughter at the other end made her smile. 'You're asking the wrong person!'

'You're hopeless, but I miss you. When do you think you can get home?'

'Perhaps Monday. You'll just have to wait a few more hours to ravish me!'

There was a silence. Kaisa didn't know what to say. She didn't want to tell him her own sad news; nor what she'd just learned from Rose. She also knew she was supposed to go along with Peter's false jolliness. It was the English thing to do, this 'stiff upper lip' that everyone kept going on about. But she hadn't seen her husband, hadn't felt his arms around her for such a long time, and she needed him now more than ever.

'Don't be like that, Kaisa.' Peter now said, correctly interpreting Kaisa's silence. 'Tell me instead how you are feeling? Are you getting enough sleep?'

'But I miss you so much!' Kaisa managed to say. She was swallowing tears, tears of disappointment, but also tears for what she had to tell him. And it just couldn't be done over the phone.

'Me too, my little Peanut. But I'll phone you tomorrow again. A few more days isn't that bad, is it?'

Kaisa wanted to say, 'Perhaps not for you,' but instead sucked in air through her nostrils and replied, 'I know. But I'm at work Monday till Thursday.'

'Ah, I hadn't thought about that. Couldn't you swap with someone? And work the weekend instead? Or better still, sleep all weekend, so you'll be refreshed when I'm there. You won't get much sleep with me in your bed!'

Kaisa could hear Peter's desire for her in his voice and her longing for him became almost unbearable.

'I'll try,' she whispered.

'There's my girl.' Peter said and added, 'I love you.'

'Me too,' Kaisa said and put the phone down.

She remained on the seat, still in her overcoat, for a while longer and watched as the last rays of the spring sunlight filtered through the back door. The wall of light revealed tiny specs of dust in the long narrow hallway. Kaisa tried to remember when she'd last hoovered. She decided not to swap her shift that weekend, but to work something else out, as Peter had suggested. She was too exhausted after the week she'd had, not least after her meeting with Rose.

She'd been on duty the weekend before, preparing her daily news bulletin on Saturday afternoon, when news of a crowd rioting over the new council charge, dubbed the Poll Tax, had come through.

Kaisa and two male reporters, one from Italy and one from Hungary, had decided to walk down the Strand to take a look. They'd had a sound engineer with them too, and Kaisa had been excited. This could be her big break, getting a live report of an historic event. But even before they'd reached Charing Cross, police had closed the streets leading up to Trafalgar Square. They had heard the crowd, and seen mounted police in the distance, and had even smelled smoke, but they couldn't get close. Kaisa had tried to show her press badge to a WPC, the only one in the wall of uniformed police wearing riot helmets who looked friendly, but the woman had just shaken her head and said, 'You don't want to get into that, love.' It was then that she had slipped.

She didn't know if the fall had contributed to what happened later, and she didn't want to speculate. She'd stayed on the pavement, feeling very dizzy, and the WPC had come over and helped her up. The two other reporters and the sound guy then said it was time to give up and go back to the office, so she'd followed them back to Aldwych.

Late that night, the Tube station at Holborn had been closed, and she'd had to wait nearly an hour in drizzling rain for a cab to drive her home.

The next day, on the Sunday, after reports had revealed how remarkable the protest had been, Kaisa's boss had asked her to write a long piece on the Poll Tax for a feature bulletin. She'd spent most of the night at Bush House. Although she'd been due to take Monday off, she'd gone in to read the special news report herself.

At midday on Monday, she had fallen into bed, and by the next morning her condition wasn't a condition anymore. She'd put the bloody sheets in the washing machine and was back at her desk in Bush House on Wednesday morning even though it felt as if her insides were being pulled off in waves. She swallowed aspirin after aspirin and told her colleagues it was a bad case of the time of the month. Which she guessed it was in a way.

She wasn't looking forward to telling Peter the full details of the riot and her reporting of it, or about the fall. She knew his hopes were up, and that he'd think she'd been careless, which she knew she had been. It was so hard to remember to take care of herself when nothing seemed to have changed in her body.

THREE

Peter put the phone down and cursed under his breath. When would he learn not to upset Kaisa? She was so sensitive about not living at the base.

Peter loved it that his wife was a news reporter and was very proud of her. Yet at the same time, he knew she worked too hard. And the fact that the job was in London meant that after each patrol he had to wait longer than the other officers and sailors to see his wife.

Most of the crew had wives living nearby, either in the grim married quarters on the hill in Rhu, overlooking the steely grey Gareloch, or in homes they'd bought in the small villages outside Helensburgh. Peter shuddered. He'd never want to buy a property in the cold and rainy West coast of Scotland. When he was ashore, he couldn't wait to fly back down south, not just to see Kaisa, but also to be away from Scotland.

At the same time, he couldn't help but feel that if Kaisa was up in Helensburgh, she wouldn't find it so difficult to have a baby. Her job at the BBC meant early mornings and long days and a lot of weekend working.

Up in Scotland, her life would be quieter, she'd be able to rest, and she could concentrate on having a baby. Peter knew, of course, that it was a pipe dream, but he would have loved to see Kaisa as soon as the submarine docked, and see her enjoy events such as the surprise royal visit.

The rumours of a VIP visit had been doing the rounds in the wardroom, and around the submarine, for a week before they were due back in Faslane. Out of the six patrols Peter had been on, only one other had ended with a VIP visit of some kind. Usually it was the Secretary of State for Defence, especially if they were newly appointed.

Last year, on his first patrol back at the Polaris submarines since his unfortunate dismissal from the submarine five years previously, he'd met the current incumbent, Tom King, who'd come onboard as they were approaching the Faslane base.

King had been a dull man, shaking hands with each of the officers quickly, and hardly speaking to anyone apart from the captain. Peter and the rest of the Wardroom had felt they were too lowly to interest their new Secretary of State, but King had taken great interest in the equipment, including the war head, asking the senior rates several questions in the engine room and in the weapons compartment.

This time, when the Captain told them over the tannoy on the morning of the visit that 'Her Royal Highness Diana, Princess of Wales' would be coming onboard the submarine, the whole vessel had been buzzing. Even the leading galley hand who'd served him breakfast that morning had said, 'You looking forward to diving with Lady Di, Sir?' He seemed to be talking about the impending royal visit, but Peter knew the reference to diving was a sneaky jibe about his past. There was no way they were going to take the princess on a dive, Peter knew that much.

When the Captain, Stewart Harding, an unusually good-humoured man, with a belly that moved when he laughed (generally at his own jokes), met Peter in the gangway an hour or so later, he said, 'This is a huge honour Peter, so make sure to be on your best behaviour?'

'Yes, Sir,' Peter had replied and wondered as he watched the Old Man make his way to the control room if the Captain doubted Peter's ability to act correctly in front of royal visitors. He'd been at Dartmouth Naval College with Prince Andrew, and had met the Queen, for goodness sake! But he knew what the problem really was. Peter had been found guilty on an assault against a fellow Officer. It was behaviour unbecoming of an officer of Her Majesty's' Royal Navy.

He knew that the joke the rating in the galley had made about his 'diving' was because the fight he'd had with Duncan, his so-called friend, had taken place in the swimming pool at the naval base in Faslane, but why did the Captain have to remind Peter to behave? Would they ever forget about the Court Martial, he wondered, as he tried to distract himself with the tasks he needed to oversee as the Navigating Officer onboard.

KAISA FELL asleep in front of the TV that night, and was woken up by telephone ringing.

'Hello Kaisa, how are you?'

Kaisa glanced at her watch; it was five to six in the morning.

'Mum.'

'Did I wake you? Why aren't you at work? Did you oversleep?'

'No, it's only just six am here. And it's Saturday. I'm off

today.' Kaisa sighed; how could her mother always forget the two-hour difference between Finland and Britain?

'Well, you're awake now. How are you feeling?'

Kaisa was quiet. How had she been so stupid to tell her mother? Suddenly, as she was about to speak, tears welled up inside her. 'Mum,' she began, but couldn't go on.

'Oh darling! Not again?'

'Yes,' Kaisa managed to say.

'You poor love. Is Peter with you?'

'No, he was supposed to be home last night, but they had a VIP onboard, so he couldn't make the last flight.'

'I see.'

'He couldn't help it. It wasn't his fault.'

Why did Kaisa always have to defend Peter to her mother? She supposed it had something to do with the months Kaisa had spent in Helsinki, sleeping on her sister's sofa. She'd fled there after Peter's Court Martial. The fight between the two officers had all been Kaisa's fault and Peter's open hostility towards her, combined with the pressure from the other Navy wives on the married patch, and the reports of the 'incident' in the national press, had made Kaisa finally flee Scotland.

While she was in Helsinki, Peter had hardly contacted Kaisa and she knew her mother thought that had been unfair. There had also been suspicions that Peter was seeing an old flame. At the time, Kaisa believed their marriage was over, so although it was devastating news to her, she'd thought it part of her punishment for what she had done to Peter. But her mother didn't see it that way.

'It was Princess Diana!' Kaisa said, trying to distract her mother.

'Oh, really, did he meet her?'

'Yes, of course he did.'

'What was she wearing?'

Kaisa sighed. 'He didn't notice.'

'Have you been to see the doctor?' Her mother asked next.

That diversion tactic didn't work, Kaisa thought.

'No.'

'Why not?'

Kaisa didn't want to discuss her condition – or lack of it – with her mother. Or why she hadn't had time to see her doctor. Her mother was another person in her life who thought she worked too hard. There was an implication that if she wasn't so skinny and stayed at home more, she wouldn't keep on losing the babies.

'Look, I'm going to see the doctor soon. And I need to talk to Peter first.' Kaisa felt bad that she'd told the sad news to her mother first, before Peter, but she also knew her mother thought it was her lifestyle that was at fault.

'Of course. But you know, you could come over here and see a Finnish specialist? They are world-famous you know. We have zero incidents of ...'

'I know, Mum,' Kaisa said, interrupting the familiar flow of praise for Finnish doctors and the infamous zero infant mortality rates.

'Anyway, the reason I called was to tell you that your sister is engaged to be married!'

Kaisa thought about Sirkka, her older sister, who'd been in love with a man from Lapland for years. Theirs was an on-off relationship that Kaisa thought would never come to anything.

'Haven't they only been back together for a few months!' Kaisa now said and immediately regretted the words.

There was a brief silence at the other end. Then her

mother replied, predictably, 'Why do you always have to be so negative about your sister?'

Kaisa sighed. 'I'm not being negative, I just want her to be happy.'

'Well she is! Lari is a wonderful young man. He is head-over-heels in love with your sister and will make a wonderful husband. He's a businessman, you know, with his own building firm. It's doing very well – he drives a brand-new Mercedes!'

'That's wonderful,' Kaisa replied and spent the next ten minutes convincing her mother that she did indeed think that the marriage between her sister and this Lari, whom Kaisa had met only once, would be a very happy one.

When she felt her mother had been pacified, and she was able to put the phone down, Kaisa was exhausted. She was happy for her sister, of course, but at the same time she didn't want her to rush into a marriage.

Kaisa thought she knew all about true love, and how rare it was – and how easy it was to walk away from a relationship, but how strong the pull back to the person you really loved was. Did Lari love Sirkka back? Kaisa thought about her own mistakes, and how close she'd come to losing Peter, the love of her life, because of her isolation and unhappiness in the naval community in Scotland. If their love hadn't been strong, she and Peter would never have survived that crisis.

She shuddered as she thought of what she had to tell Peter now. Would their marriage be strong enough to cope with AIDS too?

LATER THAT SAME MORNING, while she stood on the Tube all the way from Notting Hill Gate to Holborn with her nose stuck in a man's stinking armpit, Kaisa daydreamed about being comforted in Peter's arms. But she feared having to tell him everything.

Instead of their usual reunion routine of a candlelit supper, followed by sex, she'd have to tell Peter about her 'condition', or lack of it, and about the deadly virus.

This time the tiny foetus – she tried not to think of it as a baby – had lasted over nine weeks, eight of which Peter had been away. Although she'd already had the familiar metallic taste in her mouth the morning of his departure to Scotland, she had decided not to say anything to him. But when he phoned a few days later, while still on the base in Faslane, waiting for the Starboard crew and the submarine to come back from its patrol, so that the Board crew could take over the submarine and sail, she'd been so convinced she was in the family way again, and so excited, she'd spilled the beans and told him.

Peter had been so happy that he'd gone quiet and Kaisa suspected that if she'd been able to see him, she would have spotted tears welling up in his eyes. She too was beyond elated when her GP, Dr Harris, an old man with grey hair, had confirmed her suspicions a week later.

How she now regretted telling Peter about the pregnancy! She should have known better. This was her third miscarriage – again she tried not to utter that word too often, because she'd only start feeling morose.

It was obvious her body couldn't keep hold of a baby, and now Peter would tell her that she was working too many hours and would insist she get help.

A friend of theirs, Pammy, another Navy wife, had told them at a drinks do up in Faslane that after you had lost three babies, the GP could refer you to a specialist. Kaisa thought back to five years ago, when she'd lived in the married quarters in Helensburgh, and Pammy had miscarried for the second time. She was much further gone with her pregnancy, months rather than weeks, and she'd been taken to the local hospital. Her friend had been confined to bed for a couple of weeks afterwards, but had been determined to try again as soon as her husband was home from sea.

With Kaisa's previous miscarriages (that word again), all that had happened was a heavier and more painful period than usual, making her doubt the pregnancy test the GP had taken. Apart from the metallic taste in her mouth, which she'd had every time, she had hardly felt any different. She'd lost her appetite, gone off coffee, and felt a little nauseous every now and then, but that was it.

And now, on top of the awful news that she's lost yet another baby, she'd have to tell Peter about Duncan. And the possibility that they might both be carrying the virus. She couldn't even say the word in her own mind, let alone picture herself telling Peter about it. She shifted her position in the crowded carriage, turning her head away from the smelly man next to her. Nausea, which she knew had nothing to do with a foetus, overtook her and she stepped off the train one station before her destination and walked the rest of the way.

FOUR

Ravi looked as handsome as he always did when Kaisa saw him sitting at a corner table in Terroni's on Saturday. He was wearing a smart pair of trousers, with a jumper over a striped shirt. As usual, in his gentlemanly way, he got up when he saw Kaisa. His old-fashioned chivalry always brought a smile to Kaisa's lips, even today, when the world seemed to be conspiring against her. When she'd emerged onto the street at Holborn, gasping for air, the skies had opened and soaked her during the walk to the café.

'A little bit of rain and the whole of London decides to take the Tube instead of walking a few metres!' Kaisa said, shaking her mac, which was dripping with water.

'Cappuccino, bella?' Toni said. '*Come stai?*' he added, carrying a frothy cup of coffee. He kissed her on both cheeks and nodded to Ravi.

'I'm OK,' Kaisa said and signed. '*Grazie,*' she added.

'What's wrong?'

'Oh, nothing: just everything!'

'He not home again?' Toni said and pulled up a chair and sat next to Kaisa.

'No. This time it's Lady Di's fault!' Kaisa said. She was relieved she could talk to Toni about something other than the two awful things on her mind.

Toni took hold of Kaisa's hands, and kissed them. 'Ooh, Princess Diana! How come?' Kaisa explained about the royal visit and about the delay.

'Bella! And you have to suffer because of this selfish princess!' His eyes, gazing intensely at Kaisa were sad, as if he was about to cry on Kaisa's behalf.

Kaisa managed to laugh. During her time with the Terroni family, she'd got used to their overly emotional reactions to everything. Mamma Terroni would shout as if someone had died when the coffee machine was playing up, or Toni hadn't ordered the right kind of biscotti for the shop.

Toni always flirted with Kaisa, even though she knew he loved his petite, dark-haired wife very much. Adriana was often serving behind the counter and saw Toni's behaviour, but she just smiled and laughed at his silliness. Now Kaisa's eyes searched for Adriana. When she saw her leaning over the counter, with a tea-towel in her hand, Kaisa smiled at her, shrugged her shoulders, and released her hands from Toni's grip. 'Men!' she shouted across the little café.

When at last Toni left them with menus, Ravi leaned across to Kaisa and said, 'So that's why I have the pleasure of your company today?'

Kaisa felt immediately guilty. She looked down at the mock-leather covered menu, fearing her face would betray what she felt.

Over the last few years, Ravi had shown himself to be a very good friend to Kaisa. They met up perhaps once a month, when Kaisa wasn't working weekends and Peter was away at sea. This lunch date was out of the blue, because Kaisa hadn't planned on being on her own this Saturday.

Ravi worked as a lawyer for one of the big banks in the City and lived a typical London bachelor life. He worked and played hard, but always managed to meet up with Kaisa when she got in touch. She knew she was relying too much on Ravi, and she also knew it was unfair on him. How would she be able to tell him about Duncan? And the virus that Ravi, too, might be carrying.

'Did you have plans?' Kaisa shot a quick glance at those dark pools of eyes, fearing they might have a stern look to them.

Instead, however, the corners of Ravi's lips lifted up and turned into a full smile, revealing a perfect set of white teeth, 'Yes, I had to cancel a trip to Birmingham to meet another bridal candidate my mother had lined up. So you saved me!'

'She's still trying then.' Kaisa also smiled, and placed her hand on top of Ravi's.

For the briefest of moments Ravi gazed at Kaisa's fingers, then placed his own over them, covering Kaisa's hand with his, 'You're cold,' he said, looking up at Kaisa.

Quickly Kaisa pulled her hand away and began discussing the menu. While they waited for the food, Kaisa tried to forget about the lost baby and the virus hanging over her. She'd telephoned the GP that morning, and got an appointment for Monday. She'd decided to take the test as soon as possible.

'What's up?' Ravi asked after Toni had brought them coffee and they'd both ordered an Italian salad.

Kaisa looked up at Ravi's concerned expression, his dark eyes filled with kindness. Ravi took hold of Kaisa's hands, which were hugging her cup of coffee on the red-and-white checked cloth. 'Is it what I think it is?'

Kaisa nodded, lowering her eyes. Tears were welling up inside her and she couldn't look at Ravi any longer.

After their lunch, the sun came out and Ravi and Kaisa decided to walk down to Covent Garden. When she saw a blue dress in the window of Wallis, Ravi pulled her into the shop and convinced her to try it on.

'That shade brings out the beautiful colour of your eyes,' Ravi had said and hugged Kaisa.

It wasn't the first time she'd been shopping with Ravi; he was unusually good at picking clothes for her. So unlike Peter, who would soon get bored and tell her he liked everything she tried. She didn't tell Peter about Ravi's talents in that department, though. In fact Peter only knew about half of the times she spent with Ravi. There was nothing but friendship in their relationship, so her conscience was clear.

During the past few years when Kaisa was living in London and Peter was stationed somewhere on the south coast, or in Scotland, as he was at the moment, Ravi had become her closest confidant. He knew all about the babies she kept losing, about how much she constantly missed Peter, and he never tried anything on with her. That showed what a gentleman he was. He'd been educated at Cambridge, of course, and came across as a posh boy, with his Sloaney accent, but Kaisa knew that was no guarantee of good behaviour. Kaisa shuddered when she though about Duncan, a man who had pretended to be her friend, who had been to Dartmouth Naval College with Peter and been a so-called mate of his, yet had still pursued her. Ravi was nothing like that.

At first, when Kaisa had bumped into Ravi again, in a pub where she was having a drink with her old boss, Rose,

26

she had been apprehensive. Rose, who had been an excellent friend and role model for her during her first years in London, when Peter and Kaisa had been separated and on the brink of a divorce, had moved to the country after her marriage, and was rarely up in town. After Rose had left, Kaisa missed their weekly lunches and felt lonely. When Ravi had telephoned to see how she was, she had agreed to meet him. The first time they met after all that had happened between them, Ravi had gazed at Kaisa with his dark brown eyes and said, 'The reason I wanted to see you is to tell you how happy I am that Peter and you are still together.'

'Oh,' Kaisa had said and looked down at her cup.

'I want you to know that I like you very much.' Ravi hesitated for a moment and added, 'as a friend.'

Kaisa had been so taken aback that she hadn't been able to say anything in reply.

Ravi had reached out his hand and touched Kaisa's fingers. 'Is that OK?'

'Yes, of course. I want to be friends too!' Kaisa had finally exclaimed and they had broken into wide smiles. Kaisa wanted to get up, reach across the table and hug Ravi, but she hadn't dared on that occasion.

That had been four years ago now, and after that first coffee, Ravi and Kaisa been meeting at least once a month, sometimes more often. He also came to the house in Chepstow Place for dinner when Peter was at home.

The three of them had got on so well, that on one drunken night they'd decided to go on holiday together. The week in a *gite* in the South of France had turned out to be a glorious idea. During the sultry evenings, when they'd cooked Indian spiced meats on the barbecue (to Ravi's family recipe), and drank copious amounts of rosé, Ravi had told Peter and Kaisa about his frustrations with his over-bearing mother, who was constantly pressurising him to get married. Each time he visited his family up in Birmingham, she would spring suitable girls on him.

'I don't want to get married,' he said, holding a tumbler of red wine in his long, shapely fingers. 'Least of all to a nice Indian virgin,' he said, and they'd all laughed.

'I completely understand,' Peter had said seriously, adding with a grin, 'Not that an Indian virgin wouldn't be tempting ...'

'That's nice,' Kaisa kicked his shin under the table.

'Ouch, that hurt,' Peter laughed. 'What I meant to say was, had I not met Kaisa, I wouldn't have wanted to marry either.' Peter took hold of Kaisa's hand and kissed the palm. They were sitting next to each other on a bench outside the beautiful old farm building. Ravi was facing them from the other side of the table, which was covered with the debris of the meal they'd just consumed.

They were all quiet for a moment, listening to the loud chirping of the crickets disturbing the otherwise peaceful night. Ravi had shifted on his seat, and said, 'I am a confirmed bachelor, me. And now I'm going to do the dishes. I think it's my turn.'

After that holiday, they'd taken a few days each year to go somewhere in France together. Kaisa and Peter had grown very fond of their Indian bachelor friend. Still, Kaisa was careful not to rouse any jealousy in Peter; after what had happened early on in their marriage, she knew he must always be looking over his shoulder. However much he told her that he never thought about Duncan, or their brief affair, she knew she needed to be careful.

FIVE

There was bad news. The navigation system on the sub was playing up and Peter couldn't travel down South until it was done. Peter's Captain had been standing next to him when they were doing the handover to the Board Crew and had told him the extent of the problem. Peter's first thought was how he was going to tell Kaisa that he needed to stay on in Faslane for a few days more to make sure the glitches in the sub's navigation system were sorted.

But when Peter was about to leave the onboard wardroom, the Captain asked him to come to his cabin.

'Congratulations are in order, Peter.' The Captain said and put his hands over his belly while he leant back in his chair.

Peter just stared at the man.

'Sit down.'

Peter nodded and seated himself opposite the Old Man. The Captain's cabin was a roomy space, with a wide bunk and a desk with two chairs for visitors. Peter would have felt more comfortable standing up. Somehow being seated opposite the Captain felt as if he was in serious trouble.

'You've been selected to attend the next Submarine Command Course.' A smile was hovering around the Old Man's lips. How long had he known about this, Peter wondered.

'Just got the cable this morning,' the Captain added.

Peter was speechless. This was what he had been dreaming about ever since he signed up to the service in his twenties.

'As long as you don't beat anyone up again,' the Old Man said drily when Peter finally managed to thank him for the news.

'No Sir,' Peter replied. He wasn't sure if the Captain had been joking or not.

Nobody could say Peter's career had been ordinary. When at the age of 20 he'd graduated from Dartmouth Naval College with all the pomp and ceremony demanded by the Queen's presence, he'd been destined to great things. Soon after, he'd decided to apply for the submarine service and had qualified in as short a time as possible.

He thought back to those times. He'd been so in love with Kaisa, and had such a brilliant future in front of him, he didn't think anything could ever touch him. He was on his way up, up to the dizzy heights of a celebrated naval career. How confident he'd been when he'd triumphantly caught his Dolphins, the badge of the underwater service, in his teeth from the bottom of a glass of rum!

After that Royal Navy rite of passage, which all newly qualified submariners had to go through, Peter had passed the nuclear exams that followed and been assigned to serve on a Polaris sub. Even with the Court Martial on his record, he was now the Navigating Officer in the Polaris fleet. It seemed his career was continuing its upwards trajectory.

Peter hurried off the sub and walked towards the wardroom on the base. He wanted to telephone Kaisa in London immediately, but when the phone in their Notting Hill home rang and rang, he was disappointed not to be able to tell her the news. He put down the phone, went into the Back Bar and ordered himself a whisky.

He ignored the surprised looks of some of the junior officers drinking pints in the corner and found himself an empty table. He took a large swig of his drink. The whisky burned his throat – he didn't usually go for spirits but the occasion seemed to warrant it.

The timing was perfect: with Kaisa newly pregnant, the course would be over and done with by the time she'd given birth. He allowed himself to dream how he'd be a fully-fledged submarine captain by the time their first baby was born.

Of course, he was apprehensive about the prospect of Perisher, as one of the toughest leadership courses in the world was known. It had a high failure rate, but he knew his technical ability was good, even excellent. Peter didn't doubt his skills in the mental arithmetic needed to calculate various speeds and courses of vessels, but he worried that Teacher, as the course leader was known, might have a preconception about him. Would he try to use 'the incident', as everyone kept calling the brawl with that coward in the Falsane pool, to test Peter's psychological strength? Is that why the Captain had mentioned the fight with Duncan? Did he think his past could affect his performance on the Perisher course?

Peter didn't know who Teacher would be on this occasion, but he'd heard one or two of them could be real bastards. Peter flinched at the prospect of the terrible nick-name he'd been given immediately after the Court Martial, 'Bonking Boy', resurfacing. He'd not heard it for years now, and it seemed most people had forgotten about it, or else lost interest in the fight. It was yesterday's news, helped, of course, by the fact that Duncan was no longer a serving naval officer. He'd done the honourable thing, the rat, leaving after 'the brawl in the pool', as the headline in the *Daily Mail* had put it, and after he'd taken advantage of Kaisa.

Peter shook his head to banish thoughts of those times. He knew Kaisa wouldn't do anything like it again, and he also knew that he was partly to blame for her unhappiness in Faslane that had led to the brief affair. Peter had been walking around with his eyes closed, letting the tosser get close to Kaisa. But it was all done now, long gone and never to be discussed. Besides, he was about to be the father of their child, so even if he still wanted to kill Duncan, or still kept seeing Kaisa being kissed in his arms, and sometimes, in his worst nightmares, being pinned down by him, that didn't matter now.

Peter finished his whisky in one gulp and vowed that during Perisher, which would form the most important months of his career – if not his life – he would control himself, like he had done every day of the past five years.

Peter got up and went to telephone Kaisa again. This time she was at home, but Peter decided he'd keep news of the Perisher course as a surprise for her. Instead, he'd ask her to come up to Helensburgh for a few days.

SIX

When Peter asked Kaisa to come up to see him during a late phone call on Tuesday night, she'd jumped at the chance to see him. She was disappointed when there was a delay with his home-coming (again). Now there was something wrong with the submarine. He would have to stay put in Faslane for a few days longer, but could have Wednesday and Thursday off, as long as he remained nearby and at the end of a phone, in case he was needed.

Why that might be was classified information, and Kaisa didn't ask. She managed to change her shift at the BBC, and on Wednesday morning she got into a cab and set off early to the airport. Kaisa knew there was a good chance she could get a standby ticket on an early morning flight to Glasgow at Gatwick. She was desperate to see Peter, not only because she missed him, but because she wanted to tell him in person about the baby.

Or the lack of it.

On Monday, her kind old GP had confirmed the miscarriage, something that hadn't been a surprise to Kaisa. He'd told her to wait three months before trying again.

On the flight she'd resolved not to tell Peter about Duncan, or the test she'd taken at the GP's surgery, during this short visit. She knew that she should, but she wanted to have the result first.

She didn't know what she would do if it was positive. She just couldn't imagine the conversation with Peter. She knew he would be angry, and also scared. And, this was something Kaisa had tried not to think about as she lay awake in her bed, what if AIDS was the reason she kept losing her babies? It hadn't occurred to her until she'd been travelling home on the Tube. Suddenly, like a bolt of lightning, the thought had entered her fuzzy mind.

She hadn't slept properly since her meeting with Rose. When she had eventually dozed off, images of Duncan's face, with sunken eyes and a pallor so extreme that he looked almost opaque, disappeared into the white walls of her bedroom.

The GP had given Kaisa a leaflet about the virus, called 'AIDS and Women'. In it there was a section about pregnancy:

> 'If the woman or proposed father is carrying the virus, it is best for the woman to avoid becoming pregnant. Pregnancy increases the likelihood of an infected woman developing full-blown AIDS. There is also a very real risk of passing the virus to the baby.'

THERE WAS NOTHING ABOUT MISCARRIAGES, but perhaps the virus could prevent the baby from forming correctly?

Kaisa shivered and felt bile rise in her throat when she thought about the leaflet, which was decorated with paper chain figures in black, like deadly shadows of the paper chain elves that Kaisa hung over the fireplace in her living room in December.

TV ads showing the word AIDS carved into a gravestone and the message '*A deadly virus with no known cure*' haunted her too; she kept seeing Peter's name on granite above a mound of freshly dug earth.

She gazed out of the window at the blanket of clouds below. The sun was a pale bright oval in the distance, shining into the opaque layer and making it look like a giant, fluffy bed. She had a sudden urge to lie on the clouds and forget all about having a baby, about Duncan, the virus or Peter.

Instead, she closed her eyes and decided she needed to keep her head; the GP had said it was 'very unlikely' that she would have been carrying the virus for five years. He'd taken blood from her, and she'd signed a form to say she wanted the test to be handled anonymously. He'd raised his eyebrows when Kaisa had told him why she needed the test, but hadn't commented apart from handing her the leaflet and saying it was up to her whether or not she told her husband.

The kind, elderly doctor said that the test results would be back in two weeks' time and added that she should encourage her husband to be tested. Kaisa had nodded. She'd been vague about how she might have contracted the virus, just saying it may have happened five years previously from a man who was now severely ill.

She wondered if the GP had worked out that she'd been married to Peter for six years. Still, he had used the words 'very unlikely', which happened to be the same phrase Rose had used. But what were the odds? Kaisa wished she'd known a percentage; was it a 50 per cent, 20 per cent, or even as little as 1 per cent chance that she had AIDS? Not knowing was driving her crazy, another reason why it was best not to tell Peter. If she could at least save him from the worry, when the results of the test were unknown, surely that was for the best?

As the Captain announced they were about to land, and the air hostess removed Kaisa's tray, on which there was a bacon roll (untouched) and an empty cup of coffee, Kaisa wondered how she could keep the news from Peter.

She knew he would be distracted by whatever was wrong with the sub; that his mind would be on the possibility of being called in any minute rather than on his wife.

Kaisa didn't mind, not really; she knew how all-consuming Peter's job was. When, on occasion, there was a big news story affecting Finland, such as the Chernobyl disaster in Russia, when the Finnish authorities had initially kept silent about the increased levels of radiation in the atmosphere, and Finnish citizens had been evacuated from Ukraine, she'd been asked by the BBC to be on call. She hadn't been able to relax for the whole of May, as news about the accident trickled through to Finland from the Soviet Union and the full horror of the disaster became known.

Besides, to talk about Duncan so close to where it had all happened was unthinkable anyway. Once again, for the thousandth time, she cursed Duncan and her own stupidity. How far-reaching could the consequences of her one mistake be?

SEVEN

Glasgow airport was deserted on the Wednesday morning when Peter walked into the arrivals hall. He was early; he'd made sure he left the base in Faslane in good time. The last thing he needed was for Kaisa to have to wait around for him. That would make her irritable, he knew that. To please her even more, he'd also managed to stop off at a garage just outside Dunbarton where they sold flowers; it wasn't quite the customary single red rose, but he'd got a bunch of red tulips instead.

The plane was on time, and when Peter saw Kaisa descend the steps at the other side of the luggage carousel, he waved the flowers in her direction and was rewarded with a wide smile. He walked towards his wife, trying not to run; that would have been too much of a cliché, and would have aroused the interest of the other passengers as well as the Caledonian Airlines crew clad in their customary tartan uniforms.

They kissed for a long time. Kaisa's lips were soft and sweet, and she smelled of her usual musky perfume. Peter had to concentrate to prevent an embarrassing bulge from rising in his trousers.

'I'm so glad you could come. Good flight?' Peter asked. He spotted Kaisa's red holdall and picked it up from the moving luggage carousel.

'Yes, thank you. And nice flowers,' Kaisa added and gave Peter another peck on his lips. Peter placed his hand on her waist and guided her towards the exit.

She was wearing a blue dress, which Peter hadn't seen before. He wondered what underwear she had on and whether she was wearing stockings or tights. Briefly, a memory of Kaisa wearing nothing but silky French knickers, suspenders and stockings flashed in Peter's mind and again he had to remind himself to be patient. He'd take Kaisa into bed as soon as they arrived in Helensburgh. Unfortunately, the place he'd managed to wrangle out of the Housing Officer at short notice for the two days Kaisa was with him was on Smuggler's Way, a few houses away from the married quarter where they'd lived as a newly married couple five years previously. He hoped Kaisa wouldn't mind – it was either that or staying at the base where they would have no privacy at all from the crew and all the other officers he knew so well.

'That dress suits you,' he said and squeezed her close as they made their way towards the airport car park, adjusting their walk so that their steps matched exactly.

Looking out of the window during the drive to Helensburgh, Kaisa fiddled with the buckle of the cloth belt on her new dress. The silky dress, with shoulder pads and a pleated skirt, had been an impulse buy. She hadn't intended to buy anything but Ravi had convinced her she must get it.

She looked across to Peter, who turned his head and smiled at her.

'What's up?' he asked.

Kaisa shifted her eyes away from Peter to look at the view. They'd just turned onto the road that the locals called 'Seafront', which ran along the Gareloch. A few sailing boats were bobbing at the end of a wooden pier, but the wide pavement, meant for strolling beside the water, Kaisa assumed, was deserted. There was light rain falling onto the water and the asphalt.

'Just tired, darling,' she said, and turned to look back at Peter. 'I see it's raining,' she added and smiled. The Navy had a joke for the weather in Faslane, 'If it's not raining it's about to.'

How English I've become, Kaisa thought. *When I don't know what to say, or I am keeping a secret from my husband, I talk about the weather instead.*

PETER DROVE past their old house on Smuggler's Way quickly, and got Kaisa inside the flat before either of them could mention 'the old times'.

Inside, they stood at the window admiring the view of the Gareloch. The rain had stopped and the sun was now high above the sky, glaring down on them from a sky threaded with grey clouds. The surface of the loch had a low mist hanging over it.

To the right, Peter could see the steel roofs of the base, which reminded him to check that the telephone in the flat was working, as had been promised. Peter hoped the problems with the navigating system would be fixed before there'd be any need for a Board of Inquiry about it. That would mean further delays in him travelling back home to London.

He couldn't reveal any of this to Kaisa, and although they were both used to the secrets Peter had to keep from her, it bothered Peter more and more as the years went by, and Kaisa and he grew closer to each other. He knew it was still difficult for her.

Peter moved away from Kaisa, making her turn her head. When she saw him lift the receiver, she sighed, her shoulders moving up and down. She hadn't yet taken off the mac she'd put on when they'd got out of the car, and the breeze from the Gareloch had hit them. When Peter heard the long dial tone, he returned to Kaisa and put his arms around her.

'Take this off. I want to see you in that lovely new dress.'

But when he went to pull the coat off her, he noticed she was shaking. He turned her around and saw there were tears in her eyes.

'Oh Peter,' she said and buried her head into his neck.

'Shh,' Peter said and stroked Kaisa's back. Over her shoulder, Peter looked at the eerie view of the misty lake. He realised now what a mistake it had been to rent the flat. How stupid and unthinking of him! He took hold of her shoulders and gently pushed Kaisa away from him so that he could see her face.

'Look, we can go somewhere else.'

The past few times Kaisa had come up to see him, they'd either stayed with their good friends Nigel and Pammy, when Nigel was still based in Scotland, or Peter had rented a room in The Ardencaple, one of the hotels in town.

Kaisa sniffled and hung her head. She dug a tissue out of the pocket of her coat and blew her nose. 'It's not that,' she whispered, before a new wave of crying took hold of her again.

Peter took a hankie out of his own pocket and wiped Kaisa's tears away. 'What's the matter, darling?'

Kaisa took a deep breath in and blew her nose once more. 'I had a ...' she hesitated and then brought her teary eyes up towards Peter, 'I lost the baby again.'

KAISA TOLD Peter about the Poll Tax riot and how she'd tried to get closer to the action. She attempted to gauge his reaction as she carried on, telling him how she'd fallen, and how within 24 hours she'd started to bleed.

'I'm not sure if it was that, or if it's something else,' Kaisa said, fiddling with the belt on her dress again.

But Peter's face was full of concern, and he took Kaisa into his arms.

'Darling, please stop crying. We'll try again, won't we?' he said, pulling her away from him.

Kaisa nodded.

'But they do make you work too hard,' Peter said, his face suddenly grave.

Again Kaisa said nothing. She knew he was right, but what else was there for her to do when Peter was away?

She was proud to be the voice of the BBC in Finland. She knew it was pure snobbery on her part, but she couldn't help the sense of superiority she felt each time she told someone she worked as a news reporter for the BBC's World Service.

It also gave her a strange thrill to think how many people were listening to her in Finland while she read the news. Even more so when she had written the report herself. A combination of keeping up to date with the news from Finland, and keeping Finns informed of the world news and the events in Britain, was both rewarding and interesting. Her job was now almost as important as Peter's. She also worked for a large organisation that was well-respected all over the world.

But she didn't say any of this now; she just looked down at her hands on her lap. She wanted so much to tell Peter about the test, about the horror that was hanging over her head, possibly over both their heads. She looked up at Peter, and opened her mouth, but at that moment, the telephone rang and Peter moved away to pick up the receiver in the hall.

Listening to Peter talk on the phone, promising whoever it was to see him later, Kaisa inhaled deeply and slowly let the air run out of her lungs. Had he been called out to the base? She could hardly be mad at him about it, but she wondered what she'd do in the cold apartment on her own. Alone, her thoughts would drive her crazy.

LATER IN THE afternoon Peter lay in bed, with Kaisa in the crook of his arm. She'd not cried for long, and thank goodness he'd been able to comfort her. It was a bitter disappointment, losing another baby, so he hadn't told Kaisa his good news yet. Instead, after the phone call, they'd climbed into bed, even though it was the middle of the day, just hugging and kissing. When Kaisa had begun unbuckling Peter's trousers, he'd placed his hand on hers and, looking into her eyes, said, 'Are you sure this is OK?'

Kaisa had just nodded and placed her fingers on his lips. 'I have condoms in my bag.'

They made love gently, unhurriedly, even though they hadn't seen each other for weeks. Irrationally, Peter was afraid he would somehow hurt Kaisa, but she kept assuring him it was OK. Afterwards, Peter lit a cigarette and said, 'I've got some news too.'

Kaisa pulled herself half up and rested her head on her elbow. 'A shore job?'

Peter saw how beautiful her bare breasts were, with the pink nipples still hard from the sex they'd just had. 'No, I'm afraid not.'

'What then?' Kaisa took the cigarette from Peter and sat up to take a drag. Seeing Peter's expression, she said, 'One won't hurt.'

Peter also sat up and leaned against the wall. 'I'm going to be on the next Perisher!'

Kaisa got up onto her knees and stared at Peter.

'Aren't you pleased?'

'That's fantastic!' Kaisa put the cigarette on the saucer that Peter had been using as an ashtray and placed her arms around his neck. She kissed him on the mouth and Peter took hold of her tiny waist, pulling her away.

'I didn't want to tell you when you'd been through the mill again with the baby ...'

Kaisa looked down at her hands. Peter could see she was trying to control herself, biting her lower lip.

'I'm not the youngest to be put forward, but considering my career, with the Court Martial, it's quite an achievement. It seems someone has dropped out – one of the Canadian officers – so I got in a bit quicker than I'd anticipated.'

Kaisa was quiet again. Seeing her downcast face, with the beautiful, unruly blonde wisps of her shoulder-length hair half-covering her high cheekbones, Peter thought he was such an idiot. Why did he have to bring up the past just now, after what they'd just done, and after what Kaisa had told him?

But just then, she lifted her head, letting the hair fall off her eyes, and Peter saw to his relief that she was smiling. 'I knew you'd do it! Well, done, darling. A captain, eh?'

'All being well.' Peter said, feeling a wide smile spread over his own face. 'But, there's a lot to do before I get that far. Besides, the failure rate is something like one in four, so ...'

Kaisa nuzzled into him again. 'You'll do it, I know you will!'

'But it means I don't get any leave as planned. The course starts on Monday.'

At that, Kaisa got up and looked at him with those large blue eyes of hers. They were more intense now, and he was again worried she'd cry. 'But I get some weekends off.'

'OK,' Kaisa said and laid back down, now a little away from Peter. 'You'd better pass then,' she said, and lifting her head up to face Peter, she kissed him fully on the mouth.

EIGHT

L isten, I've got another bit of news.' Peter said.

They were back in the small, cold kitchen of the married quarter. Kaisa shivered from the chill, but also from seeing the stripey curtains, in garish green and yellow, which hung either side of the small window overlooking the steep hill, on which a group of concrete blocks of flats faced the dank waters of Gareloch. The curtains were too short for the window and hung limp on either side, neither blocking the faint light of the wet summer afternoon, nor keeping the drafts away from the kitchen. The horrible decor of the married quarter, the view of the loch, and the damp cold, which seemed to creep into every joint of her body, reminded Kaisa of the terrible few months she'd lived in Helensburgh as a newly married and lonely Navy wife. She shuddered again and tried not to think of the past, or what they might have to face in the future, but to concentrate on how happy she was now, this moment, together with Peter. Their life now was nothing like the first miserable year of their marriage.

'Really? What?' Kaisa said. She turned around, her hands dripping water.

Underneath the window with the awful curtains was a stainless steel sink at which Kaisa was washing a pair of tea mugs. She'd spotted a row of the smoked glass mugs in the cupboard on the left side of the window. She didn't trust the previous occupiers to have washed them properly, so she insisted on giving them a run under the lukewarm water. She now dried the cups, added the tea bags, and Peter poured hot water over them. There was no coffee, and Kaisa had forgotten to bring her one-cup filters, so she settled for a cup of weak black tea. But as soon as she brought the mug up to her face and got the scent of the black liquid, she put the cup back down on the counter.

'No good?' Peter said and took a large gulp of his milky tea.

'Sorry,' Kaisa said and poured the tea down the sink. 'I wonder if they might have my coffee filters in town?'

'Might do. We'll drive down and see,' Peter said. He came over and put his hands on Kaisa's waist. He gave her a peck on her lips and continued, 'Look, I'm sorry but we've been invited out to dinner tonight.'

Kaisa moved away and leaned against the sink, letting Peter's hands drop down. 'Oh yes?'

'Don't be like that, Kaisa.' Peter's voice was soft. He was looking at Kaisa, not smiling. 'It's my Captain. I told him you were coming over yesterday, and his wife, you know her, Costa, phoned just now saying that since you were up here so rarely it would be lovely to have us over for supper. I couldn't say no.'

Kaisa nodded. Oh, how she hated these suppers given by Navy wives. It puzzled her why they did it. No one seemed to enjoy themselves during these dinners, not the hostess, nor the guests, so why go to the trouble?

Peter had often told her it was important for the wives to get to know each other so that when the submarine went on patrol, they could support each other. 'It's easier if the wives have already met,' he'd said. They'd ended the conversation there, because Peter knew how Kaisa felt about that support.

Apart from her friend Pammy, Kaisa hadn't experienced any friendliness from the other wives when she'd lived in the married quarters; in fact, rather the opposite. Besides, she knew everyone at these dinner parties would disapprove of her lifestyle and career.

Apart from Pammy, people in the Navy were the only members of the population who seemed to think wives shouldn't have careers of their own. They gave no recognition of achievement, and seemed to think she was being selfish by pursuing her own interests rather than supporting her husband's Navy career. On the other hand, a dinner party tonight would buy Kaisa more time, and being with others would hopefully stop her from telling Peter about Duncan – and the virus.

'What time?' Kaisa asked.

Peter came closer to Kaisa and took her into his embrace, 'It'll be OK.'

THE CAPTAIN, Stewart Harding, and his wife, Costa, short for Constance, lived outside Helensburgh, by Loch Lomond, in a place called Arden. It was a tiny village and their house stood in a small cul-de-sac.

Kaisa remembered that Costa loved horses, and wasn't

surprised to see that they had stables as well as a paddock fenced off from the garden. Standing next to the stone-clad fireplace in their vast living room, with a gin and tonic in her hand, Kaisa listened to Peter's Captain, a shortish man with a roundish belly overhanging his brown corduroy trousers, tell them how his wife loved the fillies more than she did him. From the conversation, Kaisa had gathered that Costa had bought a new horse each time one of their three children had been sent away to school. The Captain's laughter filled the room. He directed his pale blue eyes at Kaisa and and nudged Peter's side.

'But I hear you are the brains of this marriage, dear?'

Kaisa smiled and shifted herself a little. The roaring log fire was beginning to burn Kaisa's bum. She gazed at the Captain and wondered if he was about to refer to her as a 'career woman'. In the Navy it seemed, women weren't allowed to have careers unless they were unmarried WRENs. Kaisa opened her mouth to say something, and then saw Peter shoot her a warning look.

'Not at all,' Kaisa replied sweetly, but Stewart didn't hear because at that moment the doorbell chimed. Placing his glass on a low coffee table, he excused himself.

When the Captain had gone into the hall, Peter came to stand next to Kaisa and put his arm around her waist. 'Take a deep breath,' he whispered into her ear and gave her a quick peck on the side of her mouth.

'I'm OK,' she said and smiled.

A younger couple entered the room. A stockily built lieutenant, whom Peter introduced as Gerald, came in with his Scottish girlfriend, Erica. Behind them, laughing loudly at a joke the Captain had made, was Judith, the wife of the First Lieutenant Rob, whom Kaisa had already met at the base during the Christmas ball.

During dinner, talk inevitably turned to Lady Di.

'Did you meet her?' Erica asked.

The quiet Scottish girl, Kaisa had found out, was just 22 and worked as a nanny in Glasgow. She had a very pale face, which contrasted with her coal-black hair, and a sweet smile that made Kaisa glad she was sitting opposite her. Although her accent was at times difficult for Kaisa to understand, she liked her.

'No, I work and live in London.'

Erica opened her mouth to say something but before she had a chance, a voice further down the table addressed her.

'She was so nice, very natural. The way she talked to the children you could tell she's a mother herself,' Judy, the wife of the First Lieutenant, said. 'It's such a shame you missed it, Keesi.'

Kaisa smiled and resisted the urge to correct the woman's pronunciation of her name. Peter, who was sitting on the other side of Erica diagonally opposite Kaisa, gave her a look that said 'Don't', so Kaisa just said, 'She looks very friendly' and added, 'Tell me, what was she wearing? Peter told me about the visit, but couldn't even remember the colour of her outfit!'

There was general laughter before Judy described the outfit in great detail — the Navy-inspired dress with gold buttons, white, low-heeled shoes, a matching white hat with a navy ribbon and a white leather clutch bag. She talked at length about the lady-in-waiting, and how nice she, too, had been, making sure no one person got too much time with the Princess.

'There were some sailor's wives, who had to be told to move away. But that's understandable, really. They don't usually come close to royalty, so they don't know how to behave.'

The Captain cleared his throat and, looking at his wife, said, 'It was a successful visit, and I think even Her Royal Highness enjoyed it.'

There was more discussion about the Princess and her charitable work.

'She's wonderful with the AIDS patients, isn't she? Touching them like that. Very brave,' Judith said.

Everyone nodded, and for a moment no one said anything. But Kaisa couldn't help herself. 'AIDS is only transmitted through sexual intercourse, so there's really no bravery involved in touching a patient,' she said.

There was a tension around the table, and Kaisa could feel Peter's eyes on her. She didn't dare look at him.

'That's certainly the current medical opinion, anyway.' Kaisa spoke into the silence in the room, catching Erica's eye opposite. She nodded and smiled.

The Captain cleared his throat once again, and said, 'I think it's time for some port for the gents and some liqueurs for the ladies? Shall we retire to the lounge?'

'Well done,' Costa whispered to Kaisa when they left the table and she briefly stood alone with the Captain's wife, waiting for others to leave the room. Kaisa turned around, wanting to say something, but Costa moved her along and they were back in the lounge with the others overlooking the now darkened view of Loch Lomond.

When Kaisa had first met Costa, at the Christmas ball on the base, where she'd met most of the officers from Peter's Starboard crew, she'd found her quite cold with little to say to Kaisa. She supposed that, as the Captain's wife, Costa must get fed up with having to be nice to everyone all of the time. But tonight, the petite woman who had short, unkempt brown hair, was very pleasant; she didn't have any airs or graces.

Kaisa wondered what she would have to do if Peter passed Perisher, and she too became a Captain's Wife. If they made it that far, she thought. She shivered and told herself to stop thinking about the test. Surely if she did have AIDS, she would be ill? Wouldn't she find it difficult to shake off any little colds or sniffles?

She thought back and realised she'd only been ill, or away from work, due to her miscarriages and the cramps she'd had afterwards. The last time she'd taken an aspirin and gone to work regardless. She tried to shake off thoughts of the test and wondered instead what she would do if she actually managed to hold onto a baby and give birth.

If Peter got a drive in one of the submarines stationed up in Scotland, would she want to give up work and move up here again? When she and Peter had talked about having a baby, they had decided she would stay in London, and use the crèche that the BBC provided in Covent Garden. She knew the waiting list was long, but she'd hoped that if she put down the baby's name, as soon as she was far enough on in the pregnancy, she'd be able to get a place. But that was before Peter knew about the Perisher and a possible promotion. Although he hadn't said it, Kaisa felt sure that, as a Captain, he'd get less time away from the boat. Would she be able to cope with a baby on her own for most of the time? And how would it be for the child never to see his or her father? Perhaps life up in Scotland wouldn't be so bad after all.

She looked around the sitting room where the eight of them were sitting. She'd definitely keep clear of Judy, but she could see herself becoming friends with both Costa and Erica. Plus, you never know, Nigel and Pammy might have moved up to Scotland by then. Pammy had written in her latest letter that Nigel's commission on a diesel submarine in Plymouth was coming to an end, and they didn't yet know where he was going next. 'The uncertainty is the worst thing, isn't it?' she'd written. In London, Kaisa felt much removed from the Navy circles, but decisions about Peter's career were still a major concern in their marriage. Apart from her inability to keep hold of a baby, that is.

And now the horror of the virus.

Which she wasn't thinking about.

The bare fact was that she was still dependent on Peter's work in so many ways. She missed him constantly, and a six- to eight-week patrol meant two months of not trying for a baby. A shore job would mean she'd have a chance of conceiving each cycle.

And then there was all the talk about the nuclear submariners only producing daughters. It was true that most of the children born to the submariners Kaisa knew were girls, but was it really true that the radiation affected the men's sperm so that only girls survived? Kaisa hadn't dared ask the old GP, who she knew would call it an 'old wives' tale'. Besides, Kaisa didn't really mind a girl; in fact, she secretly wished for one. But since she'd lost this latest baby, she'd begun to worry that it might be the radiation that was causing her to have early miscarriages.

Kaisa was shaken out of her own thoughts by Peter, who came to sit on the arm of the comfy chair allocated to Kaisa by the Captain. He was holding two glasses of port in his hands and handed Kaisa one.

'You OK?' he whispered into her ear and Kaisa nodded.

In spite of the not-so-well veiled criticism of her choice

of living arrangements by the First Lieutenant's wife, and the brief blip over AIDS, Kaisa found, to her surprise, that the evening did go smoothly. She even enjoyed herself a little.

It had been a beautiful evening, with the sun up until gone eight o'clock, and now when they were drinking port and eating cheese, Kaisa could still see the shadows of the trees and bushes in the vast garden leading down to the loch.

Earlier, before dinner, when it had still been light, they'd all admired the view of Loch Lomond, which had been as still as a millpond. It had stopped raining, and the sun had briefly come out from behind a thick blanket of cloud. The view had reminded Kaisa of the lakes in Finland.

Aulanko in Southern Finland, where she and Peter had spent one ill-fated Midsummer weekend, had the same majestic fells and deep valleys as Scotland, with lakes connected by narrow fast-flowing rivers. Even the pine trees reflected onto the water on the opposite shore had made Kaisa think of home.

Again she wondered if she could live here. If she didn't have to live in a married quarter, perhaps she would manage it?

There'd been a lot of talk about closing down the Finnish section at the BBC lately. Since her wonderful boss, Annikki Sands, had retired, there hadn't been anyone who could defend the work of the Finnish section at Bush House. The other Nordic countries' foreign services had long since been closed down, so Kaisa guessed it was only a matter of time. She wondered if work was still scarce up here in Scotland, and whether she'd be as miserable here now as she had been five years previously. She supposed now she had journalistic experience, she could do freelance work for other organisations, perhaps even for radio stations in Finland. Kaisa was so deep in her own thoughts that she didn't hear the talk turn to babies. She realised when everyone was looking at her that someone had asked her a question.

'Sorry, miles away,' she said.

Stewart, Peter's Captain, laughed and then said, 'We were just wondering when you and Peter are going to start a family?'

With panic rising in her gut, Kaisa glanced at Peter, who, after giving a short cough into his curled-up hand said, 'Oh, not yet. We're having too much fun for that.'

There was laughter from the men in the company, and looks of disapproval from all the women except Erica, who was studying her hands. Kaisa shot a grateful glance at Peter. He smiled at her and continued, 'In any case, I think for the next few months my priority should be Perisher, Sir,' he added.

'Quite so, quite so.' The Captain nodded. He took a sip of his port and added, 'But we will miss you on the next patrol, make no mistake.'

Kaisa shot Peter another look. Was he going to say he would miss the next patrol too? Kaisa knew how boring the extended period away from any contact with the outside world was for him. Peter had told her that most men onboard spent the first two weeks getting used to being away from their loved ones, and the final two weeks longing to be home.

'That only leaves two weeks, or so, doesn't it?' Kaisa said, and Peter had nodded. At the time she had wanted to ask him why if, as he seemed to be saying, he hated the patrols so much, he remained in the Navy, but before she'd had time to do it, he'd said, 'But someone's got to do it.' He had then taken Kaisa into his arms and added, 'And you like the uniform, don't you?' They'd both laughed and Peter had given her a long, delicious kiss. Kaisa had to struggle not to blush at the memory of what had happened after their long embrace that time.

NINE

On their way home from the Captain's dinner, Peter put his hand on Kaisa's knee and said, 'It wasn't that bad was it?'

He was driving along the narrow road from Arden towards Helensburgh passing strange Scottish places like Fruin, Daligan and Dumfin.

'No,' Kaisa said and smiled.

When they reached the seafront at Helensburgh, she watched the darkened waters of Gareloch and wished she was back in London, and that they could curl up in their small but lovely bedroom in their terraced house, rather than in the cold rooms in Smuggler's Way.

'My God, that woman!' Kaisa said, suddenly remembering Judith. 'The way she spoke about the poor sailors' wives. I bet Princess Di was glad to get away from her and talk to some ordinary people.'

Peter laughed, then added, 'Although you don't make it easy for yourself.'

Kaisa smiled but didn't say anything. She hoped Peter

wouldn't start talking about AIDS, because she couldn't guarantee that she could keep quiet about the test.

Interpreting her silence as sadness, Peter said, 'I'm sorry about the Old Man's comments about a baby. I've not told anyone onboard about the, you know the ...'

'That's OK, it's better that way. I wouldn't want them to know.'

They were silent as they passed the peace camp. It looked empty, and Kaisa wanted to ask Peter if they still did the Wednesday demonstrations on the road, but she didn't want to remind him of Lyn, the peace campaigner she had befriended. Her thoughts went briefly back to her friend. She hadn't heard from her for a while. It must be at least six months, Kaisa thought.

'You'll be able to hold onto the next one,' Peter said as he stopped the car outside the bleak block of flats on the top of Smuggler's Way. He gave Kaisa a peck on the cheek and got out of the car. It had started to drizzle and they ran, hand in hand, across the small patch of lawn into the house and up the stairs to the flat.

As PETER WATCHED his wife getting undressed, he was so sorry there was nothing growing inside her small flat tummy. But he knew he mustn't show his disappointment to Kaisa. She was already sad enough.

He went over and put his hand on Kaisa's narrow waist and pulled her close. She was still wearing a skirt and a bra, which Peter unfastened with one hand. His desire for Kaisa was mixed with a desire for a baby, something that would be theirs, something they'd made together.

Ever since he'd held one of the twins, his little niece, baby

Ruth, in his arms at Christmas nearly five years ago, he'd been imagining himself holding his own little girl, with a mop of black hair like Ruth's, or perhaps with Kaisa's beautiful blonde locks and her striking blue eyes. He just longed to be a dad. He pulled Kaisa into bed and as he kissed her neck she moaned. He undid the zip on her skirt and pulled it down.

Afterwards, when Kaisa had turned over and was gently snoring next to him, Peter thought about Nigel, who was one of his closest Navy friends. He now had two little girls. He'd told Peter, 'Every man needs a daughter.' That was when his second child had just been born, and Peter and Nigel were wetting the baby's head in the Ardencaple in Rhu. At the time, Kaisa and Peter had been separated, and Peter had thought he'd never again be in a relationship with a woman he'd want to be the mother of his children. He'd told Nigel that he wanted a child very badly, but that the only woman he loved was Kaisa, so that was that.

Nigel had touched his shoulder and said, 'You need to forgive her and win her back.'

Peter had looked at his friend and nodded. At that moment, in the middle of a rowdy pub, through the haze of his drunkenness he'd understood clearly that his future was with Kaisa. The next morning, with a severe hangover pounding his temples, he'd dismissed the thought and put it down to sentimental talk brought on by the recent birth and the several pints of beer they'd consumed that night.

Yet after several months, and two other relationships, he'd realised that despite the alcohol, he'd been right. The only woman he loved was Kaisa. After he'd managed to win her over a second time, he knew he'd want children sooner rather than later.

But it had taken Kaisa years to be convinced, and when at last they started trying, she'd lost the baby almost immediately. Another miscarriage followed, and now she had lost a third baby. Peter wondered if it was time to stop trying and be satisfied with a brilliant career in the Navy for him, and another for Kaisa at the BBC?

He knew her job meant the world to her. He remembered how after the first miscarriage they'd decided not to try again, and had gone and bought a white sofa for the living room of their Notting Hill home. It was something they could ill afford, but Kaisa had said that with them both working, and earning full-time, they'd soon pay off the hire purchase agreement. New furniture apart, could they really be happy without children?

Sensing that sleep wasn't far away, Peter curled up next to Kaisa, taking in her scent, and thought that for the next four months at least, he would be busy with Perisher, and afterwards, if he passed, he'd most probably be either a First Lieutenant (or 'The Jimmy' as the second in command in a submarine was called) or get his own drive and become a captain of a diesel submarine. He would be away a lot, so not having a baby would probably be best for both of them. Of course, he may well fail, he knew that, and although he believed he'd pass, he also needed to be prepared for a life out of submarines.

TEN

On Thursday evening, after Peter had said goodbye to Kaisa at Glasgow airport, he decided to go for a pint in the Back Bar at Faslane base before turning in. The only other person drinking alone was Dick Freely, a friend of Nigel's who'd failed Perisher, but had decided to stay in the Navy anyway.

Peter nodded to the man, who was completely bald, but had dark bushy eyebrows and a beard running from his temples to a point below his chin, framing his face.

Peter knew from the rumours going around at the base that Dick had failed the last sea trial, and had, as was customary, been taken off the submarine immediately. He didn't want to think about that scenario too much and was surprised when Dick came over to him and asked what he wanted to drink.

'That's very kind. I'll have pint of Bass, thank you.'

'I hear you're up for Perisher,' Dick said as a young blonde barmaid Peter hadn't seen before poured their drinks and placed them on the counter in front of the two men.

'Yeah,' Peter said and took a deep swig of his pint. He was surprised the bloke wanted to talk about the course. Strange that he'd dived straight in there. Peter didn't know what to say to him.

'If you want any pointers, I'm here,' Dick added with a short laugh.

'Right.'

'Though I may not help much, seeing that I failed.'

'Hmm,' Peter said, moving his eyes away from Dick, desperately seeking another friendly face in the bar. He should have made an excuse earlier, he thought. He was already feeling awkward talking to the guy. But the Back Bar was almost empty; most officers had gone home to their wives and there were no visiting submarines alongside.

'It's OK, I can talk about it,' Dick said and Peter turned his head towards the older man.

'Must have been tough, though?' Peter said. His curiosity had been piqued.

Dick was quiet for a moment, stoking his beard. This time it was Dick who studied his half-full pint of beer. Eventually, when Peter was about to apologise for being so nosy, he lifted his impressive eyebrows and looked up at Peter, 'A bit like a death in the family to tell you the truth. The Mrs didn't take it very well for a start. The divorce came through a few weeks ago.'

'I'm sorry to hear that.' Peter thought about Kaisa. She would probably be glad if he failed; it might mean that his career in the Navy was over. He knew that, secretly, she wanted him out of the service. But of course, at the same time, she knew how much his Navy career meant to him, so she wished him the best. But to divorce him because he'd failed a commander's course? That she'd never do, Peter was sure of that.

'She had got it into her head that she'd be the Captain's wife, I suppose,' Dick said and emptied his glass.

A group of officers neither men knew entered the bar, and Peter and Dick moved to a table in the corner with another round of drinks that Peter had insisted on.

The older man told Peter how shocked he'd been by the whole procedure after his dismissal from Perisher. He said that by the time he was told he was going, he'd already expected to fail. During his last attack exercises, the Teacher had taken control of the submarine twice, and on the second time, he'd seen how the man had nodded to his steward, who'd disappeared down the gangway and packed Dick's bag. It had been the dead of night, and the other three candidates left on the course had been visibly embarrassed when they'd said goodbye to Dick. He hadn't seen them since.

'All three got a drive,' Dick said drily.

Peter didn't ask which captains Dick was talking about. They didn't seem a particularly supportive bunch.

'Don't get me wrong, I completely understand why they failed me. But not to be able to step onboard a sub again. That's tough.'

Peter nodded. It was Dick's turn to get the beers in and as Peter watched him at the bar, he noticed how he still had the submariner's stoop. Dick was a little taller than even Peter, which was unusual in a submariner. The spaces in diesel boats in particular were so cramped that most taller men either never applied to serve in submarines or developed a crouching stance over the years. Something that was evidently difficult to shake off even after you were out, Peter thought.

Back at the table, Dick sat down with a heavy sigh and

continued his monologue, which Peter wasn't about to interrupt.

'The worst is that people are embarrassed to mention it. As if I was a leper or something.'

Peter felt ashamed. As soon as Dick had begun talking to him, his first instinct had also been to flee. Then he thought back to his Court Martial. People had treated him the same way. At first no one had said anything, and went to great lengths to avoid him on the base. It was only after a few months that the jibes and insults started flying. He guessed failing a submarine course wasn't that bad.

'Yeah, I know all about that,' Peter said and gave Dick a sideways smile.

'Of course. Sorry. Had forgotten about your little mishap,' Dick said.

'It's OK. What do you do now?'

'That's the best thing about it; I've now got a shore job.'

Peter gave his new friend a puzzled look. 'Really?'

'Missile Command. I head the unit up in Coulport.'

'Oh.'

'I work office hours, and have the same pay, more or less. Without the sea-time. Couldn't be better.' Dick sighed. 'You'd have thought that would have suited Mary, but it seems she was quite happy, or even happier, when I was away.'

'Marriage isn't easy for us submariners,' Peter commented, before he realised what he'd said. 'Sorry, I mean for us in the Navy.'

Dick leaned back in his chair and gave a short laugh. 'No need to apologise. I know what you mean. You've had your struggles in that department?'

Peter gazed at Dick. His expression was open; there seemed to be no malice there. 'Water under the bridge now.'

Dick nodded, 'Sorry, I didn't mean to have a dig.'

'It's fine. Kaisa ...' again Peter hesitated. Apart from his best man, Jeff, and his best mate Nigel, he hadn't spoken about his marital problems with anyone else. He looked around the bar, which was now half-full. They were sitting in the far corner, and couldn't be overheard.

'Kaisa was young, jobless and lonely. And with me away on a patrol, she was taken advantage of.'

'Heard the bastard was thrown out of the Navy?'

'Yeah, after I'd given him a good hiding. But that cost me a Court Martial and a knock-back on my career. So not something I'd recommend,' Peter said and grinned.

'I'll drink to that,' Dick said and finished his pint. 'One for the road?'

'Go on then,' Peter said.

In bed that night, Peter thought how lucky he was. Even if he failed Perisher he knew he could count on Kaisa. He loved Kaisa more now than he ever had. And they had both calmed down a lot. They rarely argued now, just the occasional row, which usually ended in passionate love-making. So why was it so important to have a baby too? Although he knew they'd be happy without children, Peter knew a baby would cement their relationship. He wanted a family, wanted a daughter or a son to bring up, someone to teach right from wrong, not to lie, or be unkind to others. Peter thought what a wonderful mother Kaisa would make. He could see her with a baby in her arms, and the image made his heart ache. He closed his eyes and told himself to stop being silly. What was the point in brooding over something that might never happen? Instead he thought about Kaisa's beautiful body, and imagined what he'd do to her if she were lying next to him now. He fell asleep dreaming of his wife.

ELEVEN

Kaisa sat in the doctor's surgery, which was nothing more than an ordinary narrow hallway of a Victorian semi-detached house. Her throat was dry and she kept fidgeting with the strap on her handbag. She'd had a call from the receptionist that morning, 'Your test results are in, Mrs Williams.' Kaisa had wondered about the tone of the woman's voice. Was there disapproval in it? She decided to ignore it even if there was, and made her way to the surgery for a ten o'clock appointment with Doctor Harris.

She'd been waiting for ten minutes, checking her watch every 30 seconds, trying to appear calm. The receptionist glanced over to her every now and then, and Kaisa knew she must be aware of the reason Kaisa was there. Did she also know the result of her test, Kaisa wondered? What if it was positive? She would have to tell Peter straightaway.

That weekend Peter had managed to come down from Faslane. They'd spent the two days cooking, going to their local, The Earl of Lonsdale, for a drink or two, doing some gardening and nothing much else, apart from copious amounts of love-making with a condom. Thank goodness she had the excuse of not being allowed to try for a baby too soon after the miscarriage.

On her own in bed last night, after Peter had flown back up to Scotland, Kaisa had woken up several times worrying about the test and not telling him about it. She kept thinking that it was the right thing to do, and that soon, the very next week, she'd know one way or the other. It was a blessing, really, that the phone call from the surgery had come this very morning, although now, sitting and waiting, she almost wished she had a few more days' grace before she knew the result.

She had discussed it all with Rose during several long conversations, which always began with Kaisa asking after Duncan (who was still poorly), and ended with an in-depth analysis of the options Kaisa had.

They had both agreed that telling Peter before she knew the reality of her situation would be foolish. Even in normal circumstances it would be selfish to worry him over a situation that was completely of Kaisa's own making (this was something Rose refuted, however: she still thought that the whole affair was Duncan's fault), but now that Peter was on the critical Perisher course, he didn't need any distractions.

What she'd do if she did have the virus, Kaisa hadn't decided. That was something she hadn't even dared to discuss with Rose. Her friend was convinced that the test would prove negative, and wouldn't entertain any other option. How Kaisa wished Rose was right! If she did have the virus, the thought of telling Peter was unthinkable. She knew it would ruin everything.

LATER THAT SAME evening she telephoned Rose.

'I'm clear!' she said.

Kaisa heard her friend let out a long sigh.

'Thank God for that!'

'How is he?' Kaisa asked.

Rose didn't reply, so Kaisa added, 'Rose, is everything OK?'

'Not really, ' Rose sighed. 'He's with us still, sleeping in the Yellow Room.'

Kaisa thought back to her one visit to Rose's large house in Dorset. She and Peter had spent a weekend with Rose and her husband Roger, both of whom had now retired early from the newspaper business. They'd slept in the Yellow Room, which overlooked fields and a small stream in the distance. It was a beautiful place, which had made Peter want to move to the country. He'd even proposed leaving the Navy and moving somewhere near his parents' home in Wiltshire. Kaisa had just laughed; she loved London and had decided never to move to a small place again, or to the countryside, where she'd feel out of touch and landlocked. She didn't think Peter would enjoy it either, even though, as he'd reminded her at the time, he was 'a country boy'.

Now Kaisa imagined Duncan sleeping in that same wrought-iron bed, looking over the same view of the fields and the stream.

'Does he still have pneumonia?' Kaisa had read that AIDS patients couldn't fight off viruses.

'Yes, he's got a lung infection among other things. They're trying out a set of different antibiotics at the moment.'

'Oh,' Kaisa said. She wondered if she should send him her love. No, not love, but perhaps regards? Instead she merely said, 'I hope he gets better soon.'

Rose was quiet at the other end of the phone and Kaisa feared she'd said the wrong thing.

'We wondered when you might be able to come down?'

Kaisa bit her lip. She had immediately regretted her promise to visit and had thought Rose would have forgotten, or rather, given up, on the thought of her going to see Duncan. It hadn't been mentioned during their many conversations about Kaisa's test.

'Look, I'm sorry to do this to you, but there may not be much time,' Rose said.

Kaisa could hear her voice falter. She looked at the wall calendar she kept above the telephone in the hall. In the next few days, there was a great big free space when she was off work. It was the week she and Peter had planned to take a little break, before he'd been selected for Perisher. They'd been planning to go and see his family in Wiltshire, but Peter had telephoned his parents over the weekend and told them the good news about the course, and the bad news about the visit. Kaisa didn't want to go on her own, even though she overheard Peter's mother suggesting she should. Kaisa had shaken her head silently at Peter as he stood in the hall, with the receiver half against his ear so that Kaisa could hear what his mother was saying. After all the years, Kaisa still didn't feel conformable in his parents' company. She felt sure his mother hadn't forgiven what she'd done to her son during their first year of marriage.

Kaisa was now thinking hard. She could tell Peter she was going up to see Rose and Roger; the weather hotting up and a heatwave was forecast. It would be a natural thing to want to get away from London, since she had the time off and he was busy with Perisher. And it wouldn't be a lie.

'OK, how about I come over tomorrow? I'm off work, so I could stay overnight.'

'Kaisa, that's wonderful! Will you take the first cheap train to Sherborne? I think it leaves at 10.15. I'll come and pick you up from the station.'

That evening when Peter phoned Kaisa, she felt such relief. The threat of the virus had been lifted and now all she had to do was to see Duncan once, and then forget all about it. She no longer needed to feel as though she was lying to Peter.

'How is it going, darling?'

'Well,' Peter said. 'First sea time starts tomorrow.'

'Ah, that's perfect! I'm going to see Rose and Roger in Dorset. It's getting unbearably hot and I'm off work, so I thought I might as well get out of town.'

'That's an excellent idea. I only wish I could have come with you,' Peter said.

Kaisa was quiet, she didn't know how to reply. She couldn't say, 'Me too,' because that would be a blatant lie. How was she getting herself into these horrible situations?

'Rose asked me and I couldn't say no.' That at least was the truth, Kaisa thought.

'Well, have fun and think of me when you're lying in that wonderful bed.'

Peter's words reminded Kaisa of making love in the Yellow Room, and how the old wrought iron bed had squeaked so badly that they worried Rose and her husband would hear them.

'I shan't be putting those springs through the same pressure,' Kaisa said and giggled.

TWELVE

Kaisa spotted Rose as soon as she stepped off the train. She was wearing a summery dress with small pink flowers on it. Laura Ashley, Kaisa thought, and saw how she blended into the surroundings.

Sherborne station was a pretty, stone-built building, with hanging baskets overflowing with pink and blue flowers swaying in the faint breeze. By the time Kaisa's train had pulled out of Waterloo, the sun had already been high in the sky and she'd had to move seats to get out of the glare. She'd begun the journey with great trepidation. She felt guilty about telling Peter only part of the story; and she feared what she might see when she met Duncan. That image of the father with his dying son kept popping into her brain, however much she tried to shoo it away.

'I'm so glad you came,' Rose said.

She'd flung Kaisa's overnight bag in the back of an old, muddy Land Rover, and was now sitting in the driver's seat, leaning towards the windscreen as she negotiated a small roundabout.

The back of the car bore testament to Rose's two

Labradors: there were dog hairs all over old checked throws. Was this really the same woman who used to wear high heels and was so adept at hailing cabs on the London streets? Kaisa marvelled at the change in her friend; here, in the country, she seemed freer somehow, definitely more at home, but also more in control. Rose had always been the strong woman in Kaisa's life, her career role model in many ways, so it still took her by surprise to see how much the country life suited her.

But Rose's words and her grave face reminded Kaisa why she was here.

'How is he?'

'Duncan is strong, so we're hopeful.'

While they were driving along narrow roads, bordered by high hedges with the occasional purple flowers, foxgloves she thought they were called, sticking out of them, Kaisa hoped her image of a dying man was not what she'd find in Rose's Yellow Room.

As soon as she entered the white-clad house, which Rose and Roger referred to as 'The Cottage' even though it was at least twice the size of Kaisa's terraced house in Notting Hill, Kaisa felt there was a different atmosphere.

When she'd visited with Peter, the house had been filled with light and laughter; one of the dogs had been a puppy then and had peed on the floor after Kaisa bent down to stroke and play with it. They had all chuckled and Roger had pulled the poor little puppy out of the house by the scruff of its neck, calling it a 'naughty girl' and putting on a stern face. He'd then made stiff gin and tonics for them all.

Rose had produced a huge salad and Roger had grilled steaks on the barbecue. They'd sat in the garden until dusk fell, watching the birds fly about, listening to their nocturnal singing, drinking wine and talking. When it grew fully dark, they'd moved inside to sit in Rose's large kitchen until the early hours, drinking a bottle of rather good whisky that Roger had pulled out of the drinks cabinet.

Now the kitchen looked cold and gloomy, in spite of the full sunshine outside. Roger sat at the table, drinking coffee out of a large mug. Even the two dogs seemed subdued, greeting Kaisa with a couple of sniffs and lazy wags of their tails. There was a smell of disinfectant, and when Rose's husband stood up to greet Kaisa, his face was serious. 'So good of you to come,' Roger said and kissed Kaisa on both cheeks.

'I wanted to,' Kaisa lied and set down her bag.

'Oh, let me take that. You're in the Pink Room at the back of the cottage.' Roger turned and kissed Rose on the mouth. 'You OK, love?'

'Did he have the soup?'

Roger shook his head. The two stood there for a moment, looking at each other. Then Rose turned towards Kaisa, 'Look, Roger will take you to your room and you can freshen up if you want. Are you hungry? Come down when you're ready and I'll make us a sandwich.'

Kaisa nodded and followed Roger upstairs. On the landing, she saw the door to the Yellow Room was slightly ajar. She glanced at Roger, who took hold of her arm and gently guided her along the landing. The Pink Room was opposite Roger and Rose's bedroom.

'There's your bathroom just next door. I'm sorry this one doesn't have an en suite,' Roger said and left her alone.

Kaisa sat on the bed and looked out of the window. This side of the house overlooked the farmland beyond. Nearest to the back of the building was an overgrown orchard. Ripe plums were hanging from a couple of trees next to a stone wall separating the house from the track that led from the narrow road. The rest of the orchard had apple trees, scattered higgledy-piggledy around an area at least four times the size of Kaisa's garden. Beyond the orchard was a field of rapeseed, its yellow flowers stark against the blue skies. The view was breathtaking and Kaisa wondered how a world that had produced such beauty could also produce an illness like AIDS. She overheard steps on the landing and there was a knock on the door.

'Kaisa, are you OK?' Rose came into the room. She was carrying towels and placed them on the bed. 'Sorry, forgot to give you these.'

'Thank you,' Kaisa said. 'How is he, really?'

Rose sat on the bed next to Kaisa. 'I'm worried because he's just not eating very much. And he needs to, to get better and to take the tablets. Otherwise, his tummy gets upset.'

'Oh,' Kaisa said, not knowing what else to say. She had very little experience of illness. She'd once been to visit her grandfather in Tampere General Hospital in Finland, just before he passed. He'd been very poorly and Kaisa had only been in her early teens, so no one had told her much about his condition. Kaisa and her sister Sirkka had sat on plastic chairs next to their grandfather's bed while he coughed a lot.

Later, their mother had told her he'd died of lung cancer. Would Duncan's skin be as grey and his body as frail as her grandfather's had been? Surely he was a much younger man, and even with his illness ... Kaisa's thoughts were interrupted by Rose, who'd taken hold of Kaisa's hand.

'Duncan would like to see you now, but I just wanted to talk to you first. He has lost a lot of weight, and he is particularly poorly with the pneumonia at the moment. I don't want you to be alarmed. It's all part of the disease. But he is young and strong and he wants to get better, so the doctor is hopeful that he'll fight this infection.'

'OK,' Kaisa said and got up. 'I'll just need to visit the loo.'

Rose got up too. She pulled her mouth into a brief smile and said, 'Come in when you're ready.'

Kaisa went into the small bathroom and washed her hands. She looked at herself in the mirror and adjusted her hair, which had gone frizzy with the breeze from the open window of the car. She looked at her face and tried to steady her breathing.

What was she afraid of?

All the literature she'd read emphasised that you could only get infected through blood or sexual intercourse. And she wasn't about to jump into bed with Duncan again.

But she knew it wasn't the fear of infection that was bothering her. It was the enormous guilt she felt about sleeping with Duncan in the first place and now seeing him behind Peter's back. But there was something else too. She could easily explain to Peter that she hadn't wanted to distract him during Perisher. 'Family life must come second,' he'd told her when he'd given her the news about the course in Helensburgh. And she understood that. Peter, she knew, had forgiven her for the affair, knowing it was partly his fault.

No, it wasn't the guilt that was bothering Kaisa. It was the feelings she still had for Duncan. She didn't want to see him suffer.

They had been great friends before – before they'd both spoiled it all. Why, oh why had they got drunk and had sex? It was so stupid. Kaisa knew she had used Duncan as a scapegoat; really, she'd been equally prepared to flirt with him. She had needed him to boost her confidence. She remembered how, when she was driving to the station to pick him up, she'd felt like a woman of the world, pretending to herself that she could have relationships with other men while Peter was away. Pretending that she could control the situation; she'd been looking forward to basking under the heat of Duncan's desire.

THE AIR in the room was stuffy. The smell of medicines hit Kaisa as soon as she opened the door. Next she saw Duncan, half sitting up in the wrought-iron bed, propped up by several pillows. He was wearing a white T-shirt and she could see he had lost a lot of weight. His cheekbones were more prominent and his lips cracked. But his smile was the same, and the intense gaze in his light-blue eyes when he stretched his hand up to her had the same effect on her as before.

Kaisa felt short of breath. She was rooted to the spot, just inside the warm, airless room.

Duncan's voice was quiet, and she could tell he struggled to get the words out when he said, 'Kaisa, you came!'

Kaisa moved towards him and took his hand. His grip was surprisingly strong and Kaisa stood by the side of his bed for what seemed like several minutes, just holding his hand. Eventually Rose, who'd been standing at the foot of the bed said, 'Why don't you sit on the chair, Kaisa, so you two can talk. I'll be downstairs if you need me.'

Duncan's eyes moved away from Kaisa and he nodded to his cousin.

'She's been very good to me,' he said with the same quiet, breathless voice.

'Me too,' Kaisa said.

Duncan smiled, 'I did something right.'

Kaisa looked down at her hands. It was true. Without Duncan she wouldn't have known Rose, and without Rose Kaisa was sure she'd still be in Helsinki and not working for the BBC. She felt ashamed. Had she used Duncan and his attraction to her to advance her own career? She looked up at the man lying on the bed. His breathing came in short rasps. With a further struggle, he said, 'You forgive me?' His blue eyes were steady on Kaisa.

She was taken aback, and hesitated for a moment.

Duncan made a wheezing sound, lifting his upper body away from the bed. Kaisa stood up and tried to slip her hand behind Duncan's back, to help him, but he lifted his hand in a gesture to stop her, so Kaisa just stood there, helplessly watching Duncan slowly regain control of the coughing fit.

She saw him lick his lips.

'Do you want a bit of water?' she asked. She'd spotted a glass and a carafe on a table by the window.

'Mmm,' Duncan made a noise and with a slight movement of his head nodded towards the water.

Kaisa picked up the glass and tried to give it to Duncan, but he was too weak to take hold of it. He made a motion with his lips towards the ridge and Kaisa put the glass to his mouth. At first, she tipped it over too much and the liquid ran down Duncan's jaw and made a wet patch on his T-shirt.

'Sorry,' Kaisa said and tried again.

This time Duncan managed to take a few sips, before putting his hand up.

'Thank you,' he rasped, and leaned back against the pillows, closing his eyes.

'I've forgiven you ages ago,' Kaisa said.

Duncan nodded, without opening his eyes.

'Dear Kaisa,' he whispered.

Kaisa put the glass back on the table and saw there was a box of tissues there too. She took one and went to wipe Duncan's mouth but saw that he had fallen asleep. His breathing was still coming in short, croaky bursts, but it sounded steady, so after standing by the window for a while, Kaisa tiptoed out of the room, leaving the door ajar, as she had found it, and made her way down the stairs to the kitchen.

THIRTEEN

FINLAND JULY 1990

Kaisa had decided to fly Finnair to Helsinki for her sister's wedding, even though the cost of the flight was a lot more than if she'd taken BA. But she was rewarded when she stepped onto the aircraft and the air hostess smiled and said, 'Welcome onboard' to her in Finnish. She already felt at home, looking at the blue and white interior of the aircraft. *I am being very silly,* she thought, but couldn't help feel her throat close up with feeling.

She knew Sirkka's wedding would be an emotional affair, but to start choking up this early, on the plane to Helsinki! That was just plain ridiculous. Kaisa decided to buck up and asked for a white wine when the same friendly air hostess came along the aisle with her drinks trolley.

Kaisa was met at the airport by her mother, who was wearing a pair of white jeans and a frilly blouse.

'You look pale,' she said, but hugged her daughter hard. 'I've missed you.'

Kaisa saw there were tears in her eyes and struggled to keep herself in check.

'Oh, don't mum!'

She'd felt tears prick her eyes again earlier, when the plane was about to land and the beautiful green landscape of her home country had opened up in front of her. She realised how much she missed Finland's empty spaces and the green forests and lakes, the sunshine glimmering on the blue water below.

Her mother led Kaisa to her Volvo in the car park in front of the airport building. Again Kaisa was struck by the contrast with London; Heathrow was dirty, bustling with people, with multistorey car parks towering above the terminal. Here there was just a simple space occupied by a scattering of cars a few steps from the airport building.

They were to spend the first night at her mother's place in Töölö, and then travel up to Tampere the next day. On the way into town, Kaisa's mother chatted about the wedding arrangements, while Whitney Houston sang 'I will always love you' on the radio.

Kaisa watched the dark, tall pine trees lining the road pass by and suddenly realised why she was living away from her home country. It was exactly how she felt about Peter. She would always love him, and with that love came his career in the Royal Navy and their life in England.

KAISA MISSED Peter even more intensely when she was standing in the doorway of Tampere Cathedral. The pews were half occupied, with people talking in low tones, but even so, there was a special silence to the place. She hadn't been to Tampere, let alone the Cathedral, since her own wedding six years ago, and was taken aback by the memories of that June day in 1984.

Trying to lift her mood, she walked slowly towards the

front of the church, admiring the beautiful murals covering the walls and the ceiling. She nodded to a row of her relatives; her two uncles and their wives, and her several cousins, half of whom she hardly recognised anymore because they'd changed out of gangly teenage shapes into grown-ups.

She went to sit next to her grandmother, who sported a black and white zebra print dress and coat, complete with a hat with an impossibly large brim made out of the same fabric. (It had been leopard print for Kaisa's wedding.) As soon as Kaisa sat down, her grandmother gave her a smile and took hold of her hand, squeezing it gently. That grip around her fingers took Kaisa back to her early childhood, before she'd started school, when Mummu had looked after her.

She remembered the many trips to a park with ducks, and shopping for sweet buns in the covered market in the centre of Tampere. She glanced at her grandmother; she looked older and the grey hairs she'd long been battling against were spilling out from underneath the hat. She looked smaller and more stooped now, and her fingers around Kaisa's hand felt cold and papery rather than safe and strong, as they had when she was a child.

'How are you?' Kaisa whispered.

As she leaned into her grandmother, she got a strong whiff of eucalyptus and something else. Then she remembered, 'You still taking those garlic pills?'

Mummu gave Kaisa a startled look and began to rummage in her large handbag. 'I've got some for you.'

'Don't worry now, I'll have them later,' Kaisa said but her grandmother had already pulled a brown medicine bottle out of her bag and was pushing it into Kaisa's hand.

'They'll give you strength and increase your fertility,' Mummu said, fixing her dark eyes on Kaisa.

'Thank you,' Kaisa murmured, turning her face away from her grandmother and staring at the bottle in her hand. It had a green label on it, with Chinese text and an image of garlic bulbs. She could feel her cheeks burn under the old woman's gaze. How many people had her mother told about her problems in having a baby?

At that moment, the organist began to play and Kaisa looked up and spotted the tall shape of Lari, Sirkka's husband to be, at the altar. Kaisa popped the bottle of pills into her small clutch, and forced herself to look at Mummu, who was leaning forward in the pew, now fully concentrated on the wedding rather than on Kaisa's problems.

Lari had a mop of blond hair and the physique of a lumberjack. He was a builder by trade, so Kaisa presumed he'd done his fair share of logging. She smiled to herself. She knew Peter would have enjoyed the joke and would probably have made a better one to make Kaisa giggle.

Kaisa had met Lari just the once, when Sirkka had organised a skiing trip for the four of them in Lapland. It had been a magical week, with evenings spent around the open fire of their log cabin, and days on the slopes in Ylläs ski centre. They'd even seen the Northern lights again, and Peter had made Kaisa promise that they would make the trip up to Lapland every year. But, of course, because of Peter's career, it hadn't happened. They'd had to give up one set of expensive flights when all leave was cancelled due to an 'operational emergency.' Peter had told Kaisa, in confidence, that 'the emergency' was due to there not being enough submarines, or staff to man them, because of the defence budget cutbacks.

During that skiing trip, Kaisa had seen how in love

Sirkka was with Lari. Sirkka had turned into a puddle of giggles each time Lari so much as looked at her. She'd wondered then if Lari, 'the man from Lapland', as they'd all dubbed him during the many years of their on-off relationship, had felt equally strongly about her sister.

But here they were, getting married in the very church where she and Peter had tied the knot. As Kaisa gazed at his strong back, clothed in a dark suit, he suddenly turned around and looked directly at her. How he'd found her among the small crowd in the vast Cathedral unnerved Kaisa, but Lari just gave her a nervous smile. She nodded and returned the smile with what she hoped was a reassuring grin.

FOURTEEN

'You've grown,' her father said and gave Kaisa one of his bear hugs.

Kaisa laughed in spite of herself. It was an old joke from her childhood, when between the ages of ten and twelve, she'd suddenly shot up and her father had said that he couldn't sleep at night for the noise of Kaisa's growth spurts.

Kaisa hadn't seen her father since she'd visited Helsinki about a year and a half ago. It had been the summer that they'd decided to try for a baby, and during that holiday Kaisa had been off the pill for the first time since the age of 16. At the time, in Helsinki, during a lunch that her father had insisted on buying in an expensive restaurant in town, she'd been so excited, as well as scared, that she'd wanted to tell him too. Of course, she hadn't. Instead, she sipped the wine her father had insisted on buying, and sitting next to Peter in a leather cubicle, leaned into her husband and squeezed his hand under the table. Now, as she felt the warmth of her father's firm, solid body, she wanted to rest her head on his broad shoulder and tell him about her dead babies and cry.

Of course, she couldn't do that; this was a wedding, a joyous occasion. She extracted herself from her father's embrace; she'd already spent far too long hugging him. His eyes were on hers and he said, 'OK?' Kaisa nodded and moved away. She was conscious that her mother was watching them.

It was the first time since their divorce that her parents had been in the same room, as far as Kaisa knew, and even though the room in question wasn't even a room, but the steps to the Cathedral, this was something precious that she, Kaisa, needed to protect.

'Keep them separate, if need be,' her sister had told her the day before, when the sisters had met up for a pre-wedding coffee.

Her parents coming together to celebrate their daughter's wedding was a moment she needed to guard, to gently preserve, like a fragile nest of eggs, she'd once, as a child, tried to save in a tree outside their block of flats in Tampere. The wind had blown it this way and that, and from the vantage point of her bedroom window on the third floor, she'd been able to gaze at the nest from above.

The mother bird had gone in and out at first, but seemed to abandon her family after a gust from the northerly spring wind knocked her off the birch. Although she regained her flight after hitting the pavement below, she hadn't come back to the nest. With the help of her sister Sirkka, Kaisa had climbed the tree and put sticks underneath the nest to make it sturdier. But, of course, the mother bird had known it was a lost cause from the beginning.

One day when Kaisa had come home from school and glanced up at the tree, the nest had gone. None of the eggs were there, just remnants of the twigs Sirkka and she had arranged so carefully underneath. Kaisa had looked down and seen a few shells here and there on the pavement.

'Cats, most probably,' her mother had said.

That night in bed, Kaisa had cried and it was only her father who had been able to comfort her.

'I bet that mummy bird is at this very moment building another nest for another set of eggs,' he'd said and tussled Kaisa's hair. 'If something doesn't work the first time, you just need to try and try again.'

His pale blue eyes had looked at Kaisa and he'd added, 'That's just the way of the world, my little girl.'

Now Kaisa moved aside and watched as her mother and father, after a moment of guardedly gazing at each other, formally shook hands.

'Hello,' her mother said, extending her hand forward. She was wearing a light turquoise dress, with a frilly collar and cuffs, with a cream coloured wide-brimmed hat and gloves. She looked very stylish, and about ten years younger than she was.

Kaisa's father took the proffered hand and said, 'Pirjo.' They stood there as though frozen, until Kaisa, aware that her voice had become shrill, said, 'Look there's the happy couple.'

Sirkka looked radiant in her white wedding dress, and Lari, whose shape loomed large next to Kaisa's sister, stood smiling widely on the steps of the church.

After the speeches and the champagne in the Grand Hotel Tammer, Kaisa sat with her cousins, trying to make conversation with her suddenly shy relatives. She found that their lives were so different from hers that they no longer seemed to have anything in common. Kaisa tried to ask them what they were up to, but most wanted to know about her life in London, about her career at the BBC and about what it was like to be 'famous'. Kaisa had laughed; her job was to compile and read the news in Finnish for the BBC, and she hardly thought that warranted her being recognised on the streets of her hometown.

One cousin, Raila, who was closest to her in age, had asked – jokingly, Kaisa realised afterwards – if she knew Princess Diana, and Kaisa told them how she had nearly met her. She recounted the story about the royal visit to Peter's submarine. She saw how the group grew quiet when they realised Peter had actually talked to the Princess.

'When I asked him what she a wearing, he couldn't even remember the colour of her dress,' she said, but her laughter was met by a wall of silence.

Kaisa wondered if, in the matter of just a few years, she'd changed so much that she could no longer talk to her family in Finland. She was relieved when she saw her sister approach the table, carrying her veil in the crook of her arm.

Sirkka exchanged a few words with the cousins, then sat down at an empty seat next to Kaisa and leaned over the round table to talk to each member of their extended family in turn.

Kaisa watched in awe as her sister spoke to the cousins about their university courses, or the jobs they were doing. What's happening to me, she thought, but before she could try to join the conversation, her sister whispered in her ear: 'I need the loo, do you want to come with me?'

Normally, this kind of request meant something had happened, but when Kaisa glanced at Sirkka's face, it glowed with happiness. Kaisa stood up and followed her sister down the hotel's long, dark corridor to the lift and up to the *Marski* suite, which, Sirkka had proudly told her, they'd managed to secure for the night. It was where

Marshall Mannerheim, the Finnish war hero, the commander of the troops that won the Winter War against Russia, had stayed when visiting Tampere.

'It's the best room in the hotel,' Sirkka had told her over the phone weeks ago when she'd recounted all the plans for the wedding.

Now as they stood in the lift, Sirkka took hold of Kaisa's hand and said, 'I do need to go to the loo, but I also want to get you on your own to tell you something.'

Kaisa gazed at her sister's flushed face and at once knew what it was. Her eyes moved down to Sirkka's middle; did she hold a secret under the folds of the white satin of her wedding dress?

'Have you told mum?' Kaisa asked after she'd given Sirkka a huge hug.

'No, not yet. Only you and Lari know so far. It's only six weeks, so ...' Sirkka gave her sister a cautious look.

Kaisa went to hug her sister once more. 'I'm fine, you mustn't worry about me.'

Sirkka smiled and, seeing how happy she looked, Kaisa also smiled, 'And congratulations!'

Kaisa wanted to say how incredible it was, how she would be a wonderful mother, but she didn't want to jinx it. She thought about the babies she'd lost and wanted to tell Sirkka to take it easy, not to dance tonight and not to stay up too late.

'Are you feeling OK?' she asked instead.

'Yeah, I was sick this morning but only because I was a bit nervous too, I think.' Sirkka smiled, 'Did you notice that I've been drinking sparking water all day?'

Kaisa gasped, 'No, you sneaky so and so!'

'Well, I've not had a drop since we decided to start trying ...' Sirkka gave Kaisa another careful look.

Kaisa saw her sister's expression and said, once more, 'I'm OK, honestly.'

They were both quiet for a moment. Then Sirkka said, 'Look, I know it's early, but I'd like you and Peter to be godparents.'

Kaisa was staring at her sister. How could she be so confident that everything would be OK? Kaisa had lost her first baby just a day or so after the sixth week of pregnancy, and here was her sister at exactly the same point. She wanted to scream at her to be careful, not to plan anything, because the little thing in her tummy was just that, a tiny fragile thing. It was smaller than the chicks the two them hadn't managed to save.

She touched Sirkka's arm and said, 'We would be honoured!'

Sirkka told Kaisa the due date was next February and that Lari had bought a plot of land in Rovaniemi.

'You're going to live in Lapland?' Kaisa asked, her eyes wide.

Sirkka smiled and placed her hand on her tummy, as if to protect the foetus from any criticism Kaisa might level at her about their future living arrangements. To Kaisa, Lapland was a bit like Scotland; there were no jobs, and very few people, so what would Sirkka do with her time when Lari was at work? Suddenly Kaisa realised that the new couple would settle where Lari had his construction business. For some reason, Kaisa had assumed they'd be living in Helsinki.

'Well, I'm staying in my flat until the end of September, and then we'll rent somewhere in the city centre. The plot of land is fantastic, by the water, and he's planning to build a place with a swimming pool and ...'

Sirkka stopped and stared at Kaisa, 'What is it?'

Kaisa felt tears prick her eyelids. Her sister must have noticed and was now hugging Kaisa.

'I'm sorry, sis. I know this must be hard for you.'

Kaisa pulled herself away and swallowed hard.

'It's not that. I'm just thinking how much harder it'll be for me to come and see you if you live all the way up in the North.'

'C'mon! There's an airport and it's only an hour from Helsinki. I managed to come and see you in Scotland, didn't I? Now you live in London, it'll be easy for you to get on a plane!'

Kaisa sighed and nodded. She was feeling so emotional. She apologised to her sister.

'Sorry, I'm being silly. I'm so glad to see you happy, though,' she added, and the two sisters hugged each other hard.

When Kaisa let go of Sirkka, she saw her sister was wiping tears from her eyes with the back of her hand.

'We're hopeless!' she said and gave the hankie back to Sirkka. They both laughed and made their way back to the reception.

FIFTEEN

'It's such a shame Peter couldn't be here,' Kaisa's mother said to her later when they were standing at the bar in Hotel Tammer, waiting for their drinks.

Kaisa turned towards her mother. 'I know.'

'You two are OK, aren't you?' Pirjo said, and continued, 'I worry about you, darling.' She placed a hand on the sleeve of Kaisa's dress.

Seeing her mother's kind eyes, Kaisa felt a lump in her throat. Several times during the day, she'd been forced to explain to her family – her uncles, cousins and her grand-mother – why Peter wasn't with her. But this time, fuelled by too many glasses of champagne and a couple of gin and tonics in the night club where the guests had moved to after waving the happy couple off, Pirjo's sympathy caught Kaisa unawares. She forced herself to breathe slowly. She didn't want to cry now, when she'd managed to keep herself in check while talking to her sister earlier.

Kaisa was saved by the bartender, a tall adolescent with straw-coloured messy hair and a strong Tampere accent.

'What will it be?'

After they'd got their drinks and were walking towards a snug in the vast cellar bar of the old hotel, reserved for the wedding party, Kaisa regretted the decision she and Peter had made to keep his Perisher course a secret for the time being. Because of the high failure rate, Peter had thought it best not to broadcast it far and wide. But now Kaisa wanted to tell Pirjo the good news, and also tell her how important Perisher was. Kaisa was so proud of Peter, and wanted to tell everyone. Now, a little drunk, she decided she was going to tell her mother. She touched Pirjo's back, 'Stop for a minute, will you?'

Pirjo's expression was one of pure surprise. They moved sideways to an empty table.

'What is it, Kaisa? Are you OK? Has something happened between you and Peter again? That's not why you are so emotional, and why he's not here?'

Kaisa put her gin and tonic onto the table.

'No, we're more than fine. It's just,' she hesitated for a moment and added, 'he's on this really important course to become a submarine captain. But you mustn't tell anyone because it's a really difficult course and many people fail.'

Pirjo's eye widened, 'Well, that's wonderful! You are going to be an English Captain's wife!'

Immediately after seeing her mother's face, Kaisa regretted telling her Peter's news. Now she'd be on the phone every week asking if Peter had been made a captain yet.

'Mum, it is really likely that he will not pass.'

'Nonsense, Peter will pass, you'll see!' Pirjo hugged her daughter and added, 'I think I'm going to get some champagne to celebrate!'

After the happy couple had retired to their wedding suite, the party went on until the small hours. Everyone toasted Peter in his absence and told Kaisa how fantastic it was that he was going to be a captain. Kaisa's efforts to say it was by no means a certainty were ignored.

Kaisa was taken onto the dance floor by her uncle, who, holding her tightly, danced a tango with her. Kaisa didn't think she'd remember the steps from her time with her old fiancé Matti, who loved all the old-fashioned Finnish dances, but to her surprise, in the firm grip of her uncle, she managed to relax and move around the floor competently.

'Not bad for an Englishwoman,' her uncle said and tipped his head in appreciation.

Next a cousin of hers, a lanky boy Kaisa hadn't seen since he was a shy teenager, took her into a Humppa, a fast dance that made Kaisa giggle. Back at the table, Kaisa had a long conversation with Raila, who told her she was working for Nokia, a local company that was moving into something called digital telephony. She'd studied engineering at Tampere University and sounded very impressive. Kaisa decided she'd been too fast to judge her cousins, and remembered that in Finland it took people a lot longer to talk about themselves. She felt like she was becoming someone else, more English than Finnish, and felt a surge of sadness. But she brushed the feeling away when Raila pulled her to the dance floor once again. The whole group, except Mummu, who, Kaisa was surprised to see, was still sitting in the corner of the sofa, drinking a bright green concoction, had got up when Lambada came on. She laughed as the dance-floor filled with Finns dancing salsa. Her family and the whole of the nation were just a bit crazy.

SIXTEEN

W hen Kaisa finally arrived at the door of their terraced house in Notting Hill, after a long journey on the Tube from Heathrow, she was exhausted.

It was a hot, sticky late July afternoon, and the air over London seemed to stand still, suffocating Kaisa as she struggled to pull her suitcase along the hot pavement from Bayswater Tube station. She cursed her decision not to take a cab; she was covered in a thin layer of sweat and wanted a shower, but of course the hot water would take at least half an hour to heat up. She'd turned it all off before going away to Finland. For a moment, Kaisa wondered if the pipes might be hot enough from the day's sun for the shower to be lukewarm, and she decided to take her chance.

Afterwards, wrapped in a towel, she stretched out on the double bed in the bedroom, enjoying the faint breeze coming in through the open window. She thought about Peter and how much she wanted to be held by him. The longing for him was suddenly intense, almost a physical pain inside her chest.

Of course, he was up in Scotland, somewhere at sea, on the first part of the practical sea exercises of his Perisher course. Kaisa wondered if he was thinking of her at all. Would he, at the end of his turn at the periscope, doing whatever complicated exercises they did, lie down in his bunk and dream of her? She didn't think he did.

From the very first time she'd watched him prepare to go to sea, she'd seen the change in his eyes. They were living as a newly married couple in Portsmouth and he was packing his Pusser's Grip, a tattered light brown canvas holdall he always travelled with. After they'd said goodbye in the hallway, kissing each other for a long time, his expression changed, and he could no longer see Kaisa, his wife, nor feel any longing for her. Kaisa saw that his only thoughts were for his job, about the boat he was about to rejoin, about his fellow officers and crew, about his part in the large puzzle that was the Defence of the Realm. She, Kaisa, his wife, had only a small part to play in the huge machinery of the Navy, and that was to love him and look after him when he was at home, and to boost his morale with letters and the occasional telephone call when he was away. Of course, when he was on the Polaris nuclear subs, there was no contact from him for weeks, apart from the short messages Kaisa was able to send to him. Kaisa had no communication from Peter until they were back in Scotland.

In spite of the heat that was rising up from the garden through the open windows, Kaisa shuddered when she thought about the Familygrams. Even though she was a journalist, she was hopeless at writing the 50 words limit. The messages had to be positive and impersonal, yet give Peter confirmation that she still loved him and would be waiting for him when he got back from his eight-week patrol. The communications went through several hands, and Kaisa knew her words might even be read by the Captain.

During the latest patrol, it had become a little easier to pen the messages, even though Kaisa couldn't talk about the pregnancy – a secret they had decided to keep to themselves. As hard as it was to just write about her daily routines in London and her family, it was nowhere near as difficult as it had been to write the 50 words during those dark days in Helensburgh in the first months of their marriage.

That time, when she'd been so miserable without a job, without any meaning to her life, seemed like a lifetime away. Kaisa turned onto her side and tried to shrug away the guilt she felt about keeping the visit to Duncan and the AIDS test from Peter. She hoped he would forgive her for going to see her former lover. After all, Duncan was very ill. Possibly terminally. Kaisa could see that it was what Rose and Roger feared, and when Kaisa had visited Duncan herself, she understood even he had accepted that he might die. He'd hardly been awake during the two days Kaisa had spent in Dorset, but something in the way he'd thanked her for coming to see him, and asking if she had forgiven him, made Kaisa believe that he had accepted his fate. How awful it must be, Kaisa thought. She was glad, even though she regretted ever sleeping with the man, that she was able to bring him some peace with her visit. But would Peter see it that way?

Kaisa put her head into her hands. During the trip to celebrate Sirkka's wedding, Kaisa had pushed Duncan's illness to the back of her mind.

Kaisa wanted so badly to make Peter happy. That was the reason she wanted to give Peter a child, to show him how much she loved him, but she wasn't even able to do that. Even though she'd been lucky to escape the virus, she was already 30 years old, and soon it would be too late to have a baby. She heard Peter's voice in her head, 'Stop that maudlin.' Kaisa smiled. He said it was the Finn in her that looked at life in a pessimistic and dramatic way.

She knew she felt this way because the trip to Finland to celebrate her sister's wedding had been emotional. She'd enjoyed being in Tampere, but leaving her mother and Helsinki – she'd spent a couple of days after the wedding staying with Pirjo in her Töölö flat – had been even harder than usual.

On the last evening, over a meal of cold smoked salmon and salad, and a good bottle of Chardonnay that Pirjo had saved specially for her, Pirjo had raised the subject of Kaisa's father.

'He was looking quite good, although a little too fat.'

Nowadays Pirjo rarely mentioned her former husband, and although Kaisa had expected the subject to crop up, she was still surprised. She gazed at Pirjo, assessing how much she should say about her father.

'Yeah, he seemed OK. It was nice that you two could be there together.'

Pirjo took a sip of wine and said, 'I'll never forgive him for what he did to you over your wedding.'

Kaisa shrugged, 'I know, but I don't think about it anymore.'

Pirjo swallowed a piece of fish and said, 'To say he'd pay for it only if I wasn't there! That was just an excuse. He was always like that, promising the earth and then not delivering when it came to it. Thankfully I was able to step in.'

Kaisa reached her hand out and placed it on top of her mother's. Her flesh felt warm to the touch, although Kaisa noticed her mother's hand had become plumper as she'd grown older. 'I know and I'm very grateful.'

'No need to thank me, that's not what I meant.' Pirjo's eyes were steady on Kaisa. She turned her hand up and squeezed Kaisa's fingers. 'I know you've forgiven him, but just remember that you can't count on him.'

Kaisa took her hand away. 'Look, I know you didn't like seeing me hug dad outside the church, but it felt like old times. You know?'

'I just don't want him to hurt you again.' Pirjo's blue eyes were also full of tears.

'Oh, mum.'

Pirjo placed her knife and fork on her plate, stood up and walked around the table to hug her daughter. 'It'll be OK, you'll see.'

Kaisa knew she was talking about her lost babies. Neither of them had mentioned Kaisa's latest miscarriage, and Kaisa was grateful to her mother for being so reticent for once. Besides, she didn't want to discuss babies and pregnancies in case she let slip Sirkka's news. Kaisa knew her sister wanted to be the one to tell their mother. Suddenly she remembered something, 'Yes, especially if I take Mummu's garlic pills!'

Pirjo let go and looked down at Kaisa. She put her hand on her mouth and through her fingers said, 'She didn't, did she?'

Kaisa widened her eyes, 'Because you'd told her!'

'Sorry!' Pirjo said and began laughing. The pills Kaisa's grandmother took every day were legendary. She spent all her days pouring over health magazines and sending away for the latest crazy cure for anything.

'She gave me charcoal to reduce gas!' Pirjo said, still laughing. 'She thinks I have a problem!'

Both women were now giggling uncontrollably. After a while, they calmed down and her mother said, looking into Kaisa's eyes, 'I hate that you are so far away from me.' She wiped her eyes, and Kaisa didn't know if they'd become damp from laughing or crying.

'I know mum, but that's my life now. Besides, London isn't that far away,' Kaisa said, putting her arms around her mother and hugging her hard.

Lying on top of her bed, listening to the faraway sounds of the city, but feeling lonely, Kaisa thought of her mother and realised that Pirjo would be on her own in the block of flats in Helsinki after her sister moved away. Sirkka's marriage had probably made her feel a little abandoned.

SEVENTEEN

Kaisa woke with a start to the sound of the telephone downstairs. She'd fallen asleep on top of the bed, covered only by her towel. The view from the bedroom to the garden below was dark, and she saw it was well past ten o'clock as she hurried to put on her dressing gown while running down the stairs.

'I didn't think you were at home!'

Kaisa heard a hint of annoyance in Peter's voice.

'I was upstairs. I'd fallen asleep.'

'Sorry to wake you, but I wanted to see how your trip went.' Peter sounded a lot softer now.

'Don't be, it's lovely to hear your voice. I missed you in Finland.' Kaisa told Peter about the wedding, about Sirkka's pregnancy, and dancing with her uncles. Peter laughed when he heard how mad they'd gone for the salsa. She even told Peter about her grandmother's garlic pills.

'But what about you, how is it going?' Kaisa said.

Peter told Kaisa the first part of the course, held at the Faslane base, had gone 'OK'.

'Just OK?'

'Yeah. It's difficult to say. I haven't been drafted off the course yet anyway,' Peter said.

Kaisa could hear he was smiling. She knew he couldn't tell her details, but she was relieved he'd passed so far. She also knew she needed to be diplomatic in order to keep Peter's spirits up. There was another two months to go, with two tense times at sea.

'How are the other chaps? Do you know them?'

'Yes, of course. They're fine.' Peter was being deliberately short, so she knew he probably was within a hearing distance of the other Perishers, or other staff. 'Listen, I can come home the weekend after next. We're training ashore all next week, so I can get a late flight out on Friday.'

'Oh, darling, that's wonderful! I've got the weekend off too!'

KAISA WATCHED Ravi walk up the front garden towards her. They hadn't seen each other for a few weeks. With their work schedules, Kaisa's trip to Finland, and the virus hanging over her (and them), there hadn't been a day when they could get together. If she was truthful, Kaisa had avoided seeing him. The thought of having to tell him he might have AIDS, and talking about her seedy past, hadn't been an attractive proposition. Kaisa realised she'd wanted to deal with the possibility of an infection on her own. But now, with the danger over, she was glad to see her good friend again.

'What have you been up to?' Ravi said, his dark eyes on Kaisa.

Kaisa looked down at her hands, which were hugging a mug of coffee on the kitchen table, where they were sitting. She had never been able to keep anything from Ravi. Even when they had briefly been lovers, he had immediately seen how much she still loved Peter. Ravi had known this even before she had realised that she would never get over Peter. She'd been so close to telling him about the virus when they'd met before Sirkka's wedding, and now she was glad she hadn't worried Ravi in vain.

'Oh, Ravi,' she said, glancing at her friend. 'My past has been catching up with me.'

He laughed. She knew nothing would faze Ravi; he was aware of Duncan and how Kaisa had gone to bed with him, so she felt safe in telling him about the awful deadly virus, about the possibility of her having caught it, and about how ill Duncan was.

But when she'd finished her story, and looked up at Ravi, she saw his face was serious. His large brown eyes had widened, and he'd straightened his back. 'Oh my God,' he said, covering his mouth with his hand. 'Is he, Duncan I mean, OK?'

Kaisa shook her head and sighed, 'No, not really.'

'But you are?' he said with the same serious look in his eyes.

'Yes, the test was negative.' Kaisa gazed at her friend. 'But it was an awful time. All the bloody adverts with gravestones on them, and Freddie Mercury looking so gaunt and horrible ...' Kaisa sighed. 'I didn't tell you, or Peter, because I didn't want to worry you. And it was always very unlikely Peter would have carried the virus for five years without falling ill.'

Ravi was staring at Kaisa. His face looked angry now. 'You don't know that. Many people can carry the HIV virus and be absolutely fine.'

'Oh,' Kaisa said. How did Ravi know so much about it? 'How do you know, I mean ...'

But Kaisa didn't have time to finish her sentence before Ravi got up and went to stand by the sink, facing the window, with his back to her. 'You are sometimes so bloody stupid, Kaisa!'

'What?' Kaisa said looking at Ravi's handsome slim frame. He was the perfect shape, with strong shoulders narrowing down into a slim waist, making an exemplary v-shape. He was still wearing his work suit, but he'd taken off his jacket as he sat down, revealing a light-blue striped cotton shirt with double cuffs and gold cufflinks at the wrists. He had a strong physique, and Kaisa could see the muscles in his arms and back tense as he stood holding the sink, leaning onto his arms. Suddenly he turned around and said, 'I'm gay, Kaisa.'

KAISA COULD HARDLY CONCENTRATE on the news she had to write up on the Monday, even though there was a terrible story about the Unionist MP Ian Gow being killed by an IRA bomb that same morning. She knew she was being unprofessional, when she merely translated the Reuters' text of the news word for word, and added Mrs Thatcher's reaction, as well as a rather poignant quote from the MP's opponent, Labour Party leader Neil Kinnock on how Gow's only offence was to speak his mind. But she couldn't think about the IRA and terrorism without thinking about Peter and the kind of danger he was in, being part of the British armed forces. Unlike his best man and best friend, Jeff, Peter had never been posted to Northern Ireland, thank goodness. That and Duncan and now Ravi, there was just too much going on in her head to concentrate on her work. Which she knew she must do.

'On air in five,' a young summer intern with a mop of

black hair and a lanky, slim body, shouted from the door. His face looked scared and Kaisa remembered that he'd only started the week she'd gone on holiday.

'Ok, got it,' Kaisa replied and forced a smile. The boy disappeared and Kaisa gathered her papers and walked out of the small cubicle that was the Finnish section office and into the recording studio.

As Kaisa waited for the green light of the studio turn red, her thoughts kept going to Ravi. How mad he'd been with her for some reason. He had left soon after their conversation about Duncan and his revelation, and when she'd tried to call him at home later, there had been no reply.

When he had told Kaisa he was gay, she had been so surprised that she'd blurted out, 'But, you and I, we had sex!'

Ravi had replied, drily, 'Well, yes, I have been trying to be 'normal', as some people put it, for years.' His face had been tense, his mouth closed and he had exchanged only a couple of words with Kaisa after that. He'd picked up his briefcase and left saying a simple, 'Goodbye Kaisa.' He hadn't even kissed her on the cheek as he usually did.

Kaisa didn't know what she had done wrong. How was she supposed to know? She decided she had to stop thinking about him, or Duncan, and concentrate on Peter. She'd soon have her husband in her bed again. She missed him so much, but at the same time, she was scared about all the secrets she was keeping from him. She must fix her mind on at least keeping him happy when everything else around her seemed to be falling apart.

EIGHTEEN

There was a faint drizzle when Peter and the other three officers were waiting for their transport out to the submarine. It being a Sunday night, the Faslane base was quiet and Peter was the first one on the speedboat, nicknamed 'James Bond'. Another joke that the sailors in the submarine service enjoyed. Making fun of their profession was a way of showing the world how proud the men and women working in the Navy were of the senior service.

There were four of them on Perisher. Peter's old trusted friend, Nigel, had ended up on the same course as him, which had been a total surprise to them both. It was an equally good and bad turn of events. With the failure rate one in four, it meant that one of the men now huddled onboard James Bond would be leaving before it was all over. And failure of Perisher meant you'd never again be allowed onboard a submarine as an officer, or in any professional capacity whatsoever. Peter couldn't imagine life without submarines, so he'd decided not to think about it, but seeing his friend as one of the other Perishers, he realised it was highly likely one of them would receive that fate.

The other two men on the course, whom Peter had met at the start of the first lessons on the base, seemed very confident and knowledgeable.

One was a loud Aussie with a mop of bleached hair and incredible blue eyes, which looked azure against his tan, so unusual for a submariner, the colour of the Pacific. Peter didn't usually take any notice of men's looks, or even their eye colour, but this hunk of a guy stood out like a girl.

Talking over coffee between lessons, Peter and Nigel had decided he must be a pansy, but decided to keep that to themselves. It wasn't the done thing anymore to talk about people's sexuality in that way, which was a good thing, Peter supposed. Not that it had stopped Tony from making a comment on any female he met in the pub of an evening or in the mess during the day. It was his constant, over-eager talk about 'birds' and 'leg-overs' that had made Nigel and Peter suspicious. As long as he didn't hurt anyone, it was none of Peter or Nigel's business, was Peter's take on the guy. It didn't mean that he had to like him, though.

The fourth officer on the Perisher course was Ethan, a serious Canadian with an impressive comb-over. He was about five years older than the rest of them and was the only one of the four who had come through the ranks. Not having gone through the traditional officer training at Dartmouth gave the man a different demeanour; you could hear the Lower Decks in the way he spoke. But Peter liked him – his large shape and direct manner reminded Peter of his best mate, Jeff.

As James Bond cut through the dark water, bumping its way through the Cumbrae Gap, the shape of the sub they were going to join came suddenly into view, just as they arrived alongside.

'We'll be popular,' Nigel remarked to Peter as they waited to disembark. 'I bet the poor bastards would rather be in their warm beds with their wives,' he added, and Peter grinned.

Although an honour, crewing a sub serving as the teaching vessel for the Perishers, as the trainee officers were called, came with real work. And often, to make it harder for the Perishers, the training took place at times when the crew would otherwise be on leave, or they were called in at short notice. The Perisher would not only have to deal with the difficult technical tasks set for them by the course leader, or Teacher, but also with a potentially unhappy and tired crew.

Being the first to board James Bond, Peter was the last of the Perishers to jump onboard HMS *Ophelia*. The guy in charge of the submarine casing, called the Scratcher, guided everyone onboard. When it came to Peter he said, smiling, 'Watch your step, Sir, you don't want to take a dip.'

Peter stopped and stared at the Scratcher. Was that a jibe at his past? Since the fight in the pool with Duncan, the bastard who'd taken advantage of Kaisa, he'd heard them all; 'Bonking Boy', 'Giving Swimming Lessons?' and 'Taking a Dip?' or a 'Dive' were the most popular ones. In the darkness, Peter couldn't quite make out the man's face fully. He'd pulled his hand up into a salute, which hid his expression.

'Thank you Scratcher,' Peter said and quickly followed the other officers below.

In his bunk that night, Peter couldn't stop thinking about the next day. The Perisher sea trials were notoriously difficult, but he believed he'd prepared well. He'd revised all that he'd learned in the past few weeks, and he'd taken copious notes during the lectures. There wasn't anything there that he'd not remembered well. He knew his mental arithmetic was as good as the blonde Australian's, and the older Canadian's; only Nigel could just about beat him on that score – on a good day. But he couldn't help worrying that they'd bring up Kaisa and Duncan and the fight in the Faslane pool. Would the 'dit' have done the rounds in the boat when they heard he was one of the Perishers due to come onboard? Of course it would. Would he be taunted by his past in the control room the next day? As Peter stared at the bottom of the bunk on top of his, where he could hear Nigel's gentle snores, he resolved that he would let any remarks wash over him. *Wash over him!* That was an apt expression.

AFTER FIVE DAYS AT SEA, during which each of the Perishers had done two or three turns at the periscope in the control room, Teacher announced it was time to go to the buoy and have a run-a-shore.

'Let's have a beer or two!' They headed for Brodick on the Isle of Arran, and disembarked the submarine. Teacher had arranged for the Perishers and crew to check into The Douglas Hotel, an impressive sandstone building jutting out behind the ferry port and jetty in the small Scottish island town.

The first beer tasted sweet, and each man downed his pint in seconds.

'Another round?' Nigel said, quicker than was healthy for any of them, Peter thought. He glanced at his friend, smiling.

'It's a run-a-shore, come on! And we're still all here. That's something to celebrate,' Nigel said.

Of course, the other three men nodded their assent.

Peter was tired, but also exhilarated. His trials had gone well; so far he'd made only one mistake in not attacking when he should have done. Instead, he'd taken the sub down to a safe depth, away from the oncoming frigate. But he'd seen all the other Perishers make similar small mistakes, and although he knew attacking was important, the safety of the submarine and crew was imperative. Besides, Teacher had told Peter that he was doing well. What's more, there had not been one comment about his past, and although he knew this was no guarantee it wouldn't come up later, it was a huge relief to him. Peter knew it was bound to come up at some point; he suspected Teacher might even instigate some reference to Peter's past to put pressure on him, but he was glad that at least for now, he wasn't the butt of the jokes in the control room as he'd feared. He'd also managed to phone Kaisa earlier in the evening to confirm the good news that he was coming home at the weekend. Peter leaned back on the wooden seat and allowed himself to think about her beautiful breasts. There were only five more days until he could have her warm body in his arms.

As Peter tipped the glass of his second pint, he was pretty satisfied with himself. He smiled at the barmaid, a blonde girl who had blushed when the four Perishers had entered the bar and Peter had ordered their first round of drinks. The girl was very pretty, and a few years younger than him. That felt good too; there was still some charm left in him.

When it was Tony's turn to get a round in, he persuaded the barmaid, in his loud Australian manner, to serve them the drinks at their table to save him having to go to the small bar. There were a few locals gathered around, with some of the sailors from the sub, but it wasn't exactly busy. Peter wondered if it ever was.

The girl, whose name, Katie, Tony had managed to wrangle out of her, brought four pints over on a tray. But as she bent over to place them on their table, she accidentally spilled a little on Peter's lap.

'Oh no, I'm so sorry,' she exclaimed and blushed.

'Don't worry,' Peter said, laughing. He began to brush his trousers, to get rid of the liquid before it had a chance to soak into his cords, and the girl also began rubbing his thigh with a tea towel.

'Let me,' she said, bending down. Suddenly her cleavage was inches from Peter's face. She was wearing a tight black top, and Peter got a scent of dried flowers – roses. He tried to turn his head away from the soft, milky white skin. He could clearly see the top of the girl's breasts, and thought he even saw the pink shade of her areola. He lifted his eyes and saw she was looking at him. Her eyes were a pale green colour, and he noticed that her hair was really strawberry blonde, almost ginger. A whistle from Tony made him turn around. Quickly, he lifted himself up.

'No harm done,' he said and pulled his lips into a polite smile. What was he doing flirting with a barmaid? Get a grip, he thought and sat down again, not looking at Tony or the girl. The barmaid, Katie, now even more red in the face, moved away, muttering 'Sorry.'

'It's fine,' Peter said, trying to smile in a polite, and not at all flirtatious way.

When the girl had gone back to her station behind the bar, Peter turned to Nigel, 'So, did you get hold of Pammy?'

'Wow, wow, wow!' Tony said instead, ignoring Nigel.

He got up and patted Peter on the back, 'You're in there, mate.'

'She's a good-looking lass,' Ethan said. He lifted his pint up, 'Enjoy it while it lasts; you'll soon become invisible to that kind of totty.' Ethan was grinning, stroking the few hairs on top of his head, which were neatly arranged in an attempt to cover the large bald patch.

'Not me, I'm a happily married man,' Peter said, glancing at Nigel, then lifting his pint and smiling at Ethan and Tony in turn. 'So be my guest, Tony,' he added, lifting his eyebrows and nodding at Nigel.

Nigel looked down at his pint and tried to suppress a smile.

For a moment no one spoke. Finally Tony, looking flustered, and addressing Peter, said, 'Not what I heard, mate.'

Peter stared at the Aussie.

'That's enough, Tony,' Nigel said. Peter's friend was speaking while shaking his head, without looking in Tony's direction.

Ethan was sitting still, watching Peter. *He knows too*, Peter thought.

No one spoke for a moment.

'To answer your question, Peter. Yes, I did get hold of Pammy and she sends her love. Can't wait to see her and the girls,' Nigel said, breaking the silent tension.

But the Aussie wouldn't let it be. 'You might as well, don't you think, Bonkie?'

Peter looked at Tony. Then he forced a smile. That nickname had enraged him each time he'd heard it after the Court Martial, and even though he'd got used it, it still hurt. But he needed to keep his head.

'Tony,' Nigel said. There was a warning in Peter's friend's voice.

'I mean, your wife is probably at it as we speak?'

Peter looked down at his beer and tried to concentrate on his breathing. He didn't trust himself to look at Tony or Nigel, or Ethan for that matter.

Suddenly, after what seemed to Peter like several minutes, he felt Nigel's hand on his shoulder. Then he heard a forced laughter from his friend. 'You're not married are you, Tony?'

'No, mate, don't need the trouble!' Tony replied. Peter was newly annoyed by the arrogance in his loud voice.

Peter lifted his head. Keeping his eyes steadily on Tony's, he said, 'So why don't you see if you can have a go at our lovely barmaid yourself then, Tony? I'm sure she'll not be able to resist your Aussie charms.' Peter glanced at Nigel, who was sitting next to him.

Tony shifted in his seat and brushed back his golden locks. 'Nah, I think I'll try to get into my bunk early tonight. It's been a tough week, eh?' His tone was more conciliatory now.

'Perhaps she's not your type?' Peter continued, even though he saw that Nigel gave him a look of warning.

'What do you mean, mate?'

Peter took a swig out of his beer, 'Well, perhaps you fancy a girl who's got a slimmer figure, a flatter chest and perhaps a bit more down there, you know?' Peter pointed towards Tony's crutch.

At these words, Tony got up and slammed his now empty pint onto the table. 'Look here ...'

But he didn't have time to finish his sentence. They saw the large, now all too familiar shape of Teacher approach the far corner of the bar where they were sitting.

'How are we doing? Can I get you a round?' the man,

with his bulky, authoritative shape was looking at each Perisher in turn.

Tony had sat back down and now said, 'Yes, thank you, Sir, very kind.'

The others, including Peter, murmured their thanks and as Teacher left them to order the drinks, Nigel spoke. 'Listen you two. I don't need to tell you how stupid you are being, do I? Stuff like that could get you both thrown out in a jiffy, and that's not what either of you want now, is it?'

Peter looked at his friend. It was as if Teacher had just thrown cold water over Peter's head and woken him up to the real world. *I'm being stupid. As stupid as I was when I started that bloody fight with Duncan all those years ago. I'm better than this bloody Aussie.*

Peter emptied his glass and glanced across the table at the Australian. Lifting his empty pint up, he said, 'No hard feelings, eh?'

'Yeah, right,' Tony said and got up. 'Any idea where the heads are?'

Nigel pointed Tony towards the men's loos, took a deep breath, and leaned back onto the sofa.

'Well, I'd better give Teacher a hand at the bar,' Ethan said and got up.

'What the hell?' Nigel said to Peter when the older man was out of hearing distance. His face was inches from Peter's and his eyes black with anger. 'What the fuck did you think you were doing?'

'Yeah, I know, I shouldn't have, but everyone knows he's a poofter and that stuff about Kaisa really got to me.' Peter replied.

'Well don't let it. Calling him out won't do you any good whatsoever. Besides, what does it really matter anymore?' Nigel finished the dregs of his beer, and seeing Teacher and

Ethan approach with the refills, said, 'Get your head straight, Peter, or I'll throw you overboard myself.'

WHEN PETER and the other Perishers got back to the base at Faslane, after another gruelling week at sea, they immediately headed for the Back Bar. Peter knew Nigel was expected at home at the Smuggler's Way married patch, where he'd moved his family just days before the start of the Perisher course. But he'd agreed to one pint with Peter, who had to wait until the next morning to fly back to Kaisa in London. While chatting, the two men were approached by an old engineering mate of theirs called Bernie. Peter greeted the man, now almost completely grey, and asked if he would like a refill of his empty pint of beer.

'Sure,' he replied and settled himself between Nigel and Peter.

Peter ordered another round and they toasted each other.

'How's it going?' Bernie asked, presumably meaning Perisher. Peter nodded and Nigel said, 'Haven't sunk a single submarine or ship yet, so that's a positive.'

The all laughed at the joke, and then asked after each other's wives. The women had lived in the married quarters when the three men served in HMS *Restless*. Peter looked down at his glass, thinking Bernie didn't bring back good memories.

'I wanted to tell you before you heard it through the grapevine,' Bernie suddenly said, leaning towards Peter and lowering his voice.

Peter looked at the engineer. His eyes had gone grey too, to match his thinning hair. He had a few years on Peter, perhaps five, and made Peter think, *Do I look that old too?*

He'd noticed that his own hair was becoming more salt than pepper. An image of his father, who now had a mop of pure white hair, flashed through Peter's mind.

'Duncan has passed away.'

'Excuse me?' Peter said, thinking he hadn't heard right.

'Oh my God. What happened?' Nigel asked. He placed his pint on the bar and glanced along it to see where the steward serving behind the bar was. Luckily he was wiping glasses at the far end, while watching a small TV set fixed onto the corner of the room.

'Well, he died of pneumonia, but it was really ...' Bernie glanced around and leaned in to whisper to the two men, 'AIDS.'

Peter stared at Bernie, unable to say anything. Duncan had AIDS! Duncan was a shirt-lifter? That couldn't be! Why, in that case, would he have gone after Kaisa? Kaisa! Peter put his hand over his mouth, placed his pint on the bar and steadied himself with his hand.

'What the hell, Kaisa?'

Kaisa took a deep breath. She could hear Peter had been drinking. When he'd first phoned her and told her the terrible news about Duncan, Kaisa had been quiet. She'd had the phone call from Rose the night before and had shed a few tears for poor Duncan over the phone with her friend. Soon Peter had realised that Kaisa already knew, and had known for some time about Duncan's condition.

'I didn't want to tell you because ...'

'Yes, now, what would the reason be?' Peter said. 'I am extremely interested to hear it!' He was whispering loudly down the phone. She knew he was worried about being overheard. His strangled whispering sounded so angry that

Kaisa didn't know what to say. Not since the aftermath of the fight with Duncan had Peter been so livid with her.

'Because I knew you'd be like this,' Kaisa said quietly.

Peter didn't reply.

'But I told you, I'm not HIV positive, and neither will you be.'

'Well, I'm glad to hear it,' Peter said, now using his normal voice. 'It might have been prudent of you to let me know about this whole affair a bit sooner!' he said drily in a loud voice, no longer caring who in the wardroom might hear him.

'Can we talk about this when you're back at home?' Kaisa said, in what she hoped was a conciliatory tone.

'OK,' Peter said and hung up. He hadn't even told her what flight he was booked on the next morning.

Kaisa went into the lounge, flicked the telly on and tried to calm down. The ten o'clock news was just about to start and the gongs of Big Ben rang in her ears and jangled her nerves.

She stood up, turned the sound down and sat back on the sofa. Kaisa took a deep breath and exhaled slowly. It was as if all the sneaking around, the relief over the negative test result months before and the new grief for Duncan hit her at the same time. She understood why Peter was angry; she'd been angry herself when Rose had told her about the AIDS virus.

Even at the best of times, Kaisa hated these rows they had over the telephone. You could never really hear what the other was saying, let alone thinking. She knew she should have told Peter earlier about Duncan and the possibility of her carrying the virus. She knew it was a big deal, especially as she was trying for a baby, however much Rose had tried to convince her that it was highly unlikely she would have contracted it five years ago. She'd told Kaisa that Duncan hadn't been sleeping around that much when he was in the Navy, not compared with afterwards. Kaisa had no idea you could get AIDS if you weren't gay, which Rose insisted Duncan wasn't.

But she also knew that she'd kept a huge secret from her husband, while he was still on Perisher and needed to concentrate on the course. Just thinking about having to tell the whole sorry story to Peter set her heart pounding. It had been right not to tell Peter about the test and the possibility that Kaisa – and Peter – might be infected with AIDS, but at the same time, keeping such a huge secret had been dishonest.

Kaisa put her head into her hands. And now Duncan had died. At least she had seen him, and even though she hadn't actually spoken to him much, because he had been so poorly and struggling to breathe, let alone have a conversation, she believed those few words, and the fact that she'd told Duncan she'd forgiven him, made him understand that she still cared for him as a friend. If only she could make Peter see that.

But her thoughts quickly returned to Rose. Getting up again, she dialled her friend's number. She waited for several rings, but there was no answer. Then she looked at her watch and realised it was too late to call anyone and replaced the receiver on its hook. Poor Rose would be organising the funeral, she thought, and Kaisa suddenly knew she wanted to go. She decided to write her friend a note. She picked up some blue Basildon Bond paper and the fountain pen Peter always used for official Navy correspondence, and began to write.

NINETEEN

Peter looked tired when he stepped out of the black cab outside their house on Chepstow Place. He hadn't shaved and his jaw was dark with stubble, making him look like an old sea dog, which Kaisa supposed he was. He was carrying his battered, old Pusser's Grip. The cream coloured canvas of the holdall had dark patches at the corners.

Kaisa wanted to run to him and put his arms around Peter's neck, but she wasn't sure how angry he was. Besides, the neighbours might see her and she knew how he hated that kind of public show of emotion, so she stood at the door and smiled at him while Peter took the few steps along the front garden.

It only took one look, and she was in his warm embrace. She could tell he'd forgiven her and had really missed her, this time by the force of his arms around her and the way he pressed his hips against hers.

'Take your skis off first,' Kaisa joked.

'What?' Peter pulled back and stared down at Kaisa.

Close up, she could see his eyes were bloodshot and the stubble on his chin was older than just one day's growth.

'Oh, an old Finnish joke. The soldiers coming home from the Winter War didn't take their skis off before ...'

Peter closed the door behind him and, taking her hand, pulled her up the stairs.

AFTERWARDS THEY LAY in each other's arms listening to the evening chorus of the birds in the garden.

Peter took Kaisa's face between his hands and kissed her lips. 'I've missed you.'

'I gathered,' Kaisa smiled and laid her head on Peter's shoulder.

They were both quiet for a moment. Then, because she knew she must broach the subject, Kaisa, choosing her words carefully, said, 'I'm sorry, but I didn't want you to worry while you were on Perisher ...'

Kaisa could feel Peter's body tense underneath her. She wondered if she'd made a mistake talking about it now, so soon after their love-making.

Peter lifted himself up, and sat at the edge of the bed, his back to Kaisa. His shoulder lifted as he inhaled deeply and let the air out slowly.

'OK, let me have the whole story,' he said.

'Can you look at me, Peter, please?'

Her husband turned his head around and Kaisa, grabbing the duvet, climbed over to sit next to him. She wrapped some of it over Peter, and sitting like that, side by side, Kaisa told him the whole sorry tale of how Rose had broken the news of the virus, and how she had taken the test, nervously waited for it, while keeping Peter in the dark. She also told him about Duncan, and how ill he'd been, and how he'd asked to see her.

'And you went,' Peter said, lifting his head and looking directly at Kaisa. His eyes were sad, and his face had a resigned look.

'Yes.'

'Right,' Peter said.

'I'm sorry, but now he's gone, I'm glad I did,' Kaisa said, looking down at her hands.

Peter was quiet and Kaisa was afraid to say anymore. Whatever she had imagined, the many scenarios of how she was going to tell Peter everything, none of it was as bad as his silence was now.

Peter shifted a little and Kaisa imagined he was gong to get up and leave her there, hanging, too angry to speak to her. Instead, he put his arms around Kaisa and said into her ear, 'I agree.'

Kaisa's relief was palpable. It was as if a great weight that had been pressing down on her chest had been lifted off. She searched Peter's mouth and was surprised to find that there were tears running down his face. She'd never seen him cry before.

'Oh, Peter, I'm so sorry.'

'No, I should be sorry. You poor darling, having to keep all of this from me, and then I act like a complete ass.'

They kissed for a long time, and then hugged each other, Kaisa rocking Peter on the edge of the bed.

'It's OK,' she kept saying over and over.

AFTER LYING in bed for what seemed like hours, Kaisa put her head on Peter's shoulder and said, 'Are you now going to tell me how it's going?'

Peter got up and began searching for his cigarettes. As he looked in the pockets of his trousers, Kaisa admired his tall, muscular back, but noticed that there was a tiny bit of loose fat around his hips that she hadn't noticed before. *We're both getting older,* she thought. *Soon it'll be too late for us to have a child.*

'So?' she said when Peter had got back into bed, sitting up against the pillows, smoking his cigarette.

'It's hard, but I think I'm doing OK,' Peter said, blowing the smoke away from Kaisa and out of the window he'd cracked open after finding the packet of Marlboros in his Pusser's Grip.

'You'll soon have to give that up when you're with me, if I ...'

Peter put his arm around Kaisa's shoulders and kissed the top of her head. 'I know, Peanut.' He straightened himself up and said, 'Are we trying again? I didn't think ... should I have worn a jacket?'

Kaisa smiled, 'No, that's fine, we can try again. It's been three months.'

Peter stubbed out his cigarette on a saucer he'd found on the bedside table and turned his face towards Kaisa's. He took her hand between his and said, 'Are you sure?'

Kaisa looked down at Peter's hands. His fingers were long, and there were a few dark hairs between the knuckles and on the back of the hand. Her own hands between his looked small and childlike.

'I'm fine; besides, it's been more than three months.' Kaisa smiled at Peter and he grinned back. 'We'll just have to make this weekend count then, won't we?'

He took Kaisa into his arms once again and kissed the back of her neck.

It wasn't until they were having breakfast the next morning that Kaisa felt she could broach the subject of Duncan's funeral.

'I spoke to Rose,' Kaisa said. She'd phoned Kaisa back an hour after she'd finished the letter. Rose had been tearful, and upset, but had told Kaisa that she and Peter would be more than welcome to attend the service, which was to be held at their local church on Saturday.

'The funeral is tomorrow. We might want to go? You don't need to go back until Sunday, and we could drive there and back in a day?'

Peter sat at the table, with the *Telegraph* open on his lap, 'You are serious?' He looked at Kaisa with an expression that she couldn't decipher.

Kaisa looked at her hands, 'You were at Dartmouth together. And friends, until ...'

Peter was gazing at her. 'You never told me what he said when you saw him.'

Kaisa lifted her head and looked directly at her husband. 'He was really too ill to speak. He had pneumonia and struggled to breathe, let alone talk.' She felt her voice falter and tears prick her eyes. 'But he asked for my forgiveness and I said that I had forgotten about it long ago.'

Peter got up and put his arms around Kaisa. 'That must have been awful.'

Kaisa let herself cry then, tears that she had been holding back for what seemed like months.

'Rose said we should go, "For a show of absolution all around",' Kaisa said, quoting her friend between sobs.

Peter put his hand on Kaisa's chin and lifted her face up to his. He wiped her tears away with a tissue and said, 'Is that what you really want?'

'I think it's the right thing to do,' Kaisa replied.

TWENTY

The church was a small, ancient building with a lychgate. In the graveyard, the old stone headstones were covered with moss and leaning this way and that.

Kaisa and Peter joined the queue of people making their way slowly along a narrow path leading to the entrance. Kaisa saw Rose standing there, with Roger and another, older man, who looked a little like Duncan. She presumed this was Duncan's uncle. Two women, about the same age as Rose, stood on the opposite side of the door. One had a mop of blonde hair swept back in a stylish chignon, the other a short bob, also blonde. Kaisa guessed these were Duncan's other cousins. The hair and facial features of the two women reminded Kaisa of Duncan, while his uncle had the same tall frame, and hunched his shoulders in the same manner. Kaisa shivered and squeezed closer to Peter, slipping her arm in the crook of his.

'You OK?' Peter said and placed his hand on the sleeve of Kaisa's black blazer.

Kaisa looked up at his face and nodded. She was

already fighting tears and the service hadn't even started yet.

When it was their turn to greet Duncan's family, Rose made the introductions, saying Peter and Kaisa were 'friends from Duncan's Navy days.' There was a flicker of recognition at the mention of their surname in the face of the woman with the short bob, but the women both just muttered, 'Thank you for coming,' shaking their hands briefly before moving onto the person behind them.

Kaisa and Peter found a seat at the back of the church. A short while after they'd settled down, Rose came up and whispered to Kaisa, 'There's food and drinks at the pub opposite afterwards. I'd be very glad if you could stay?'

'We'll see,' Kaisa said and glanced sideways at Peter. Rose nodded, and Kaisa squeezed her friend's hand, 'You OK?' Rose pulled her mouth into a smile, but Kaisa could see there were tears forming in her eyes. 'See you later, perhaps?' Rose said and made her way towards the front of the small church.

It was a brief service, and Kaisa was struck how, instead of mourning the recently passed, as was the custom in Finland, the aim seemed to be to celebrate the life of the deceased. Rose spoke beautifully about her 'infuriatingly charming' cousin, something Kaisa could recognise. She was thinking back to when she had seen him a few weeks before, lying in the bed, still smiling at her when she'd said goodbye to him. Had he known he was close to death then?

Duncan's uncle said a few words about how his nephew had become a brilliant farmer, and how he loved the land he'd been raised on. Kaisa tried to remember if his parents were alive, because there wasn't anyone of that age group, apart from his uncle, sitting in the front pews. She presumed they were either too distraught or too old to attend the funeral.

Kaisa's thoughts went back to Matti's funeral, which she now believed she should never have attended. She couldn't comprehend that this was the second funeral of a man she'd been intimate with. Was it something to do with her? Was she the kiss of death? Kaisa shrugged away such stupid thoughts. Today was nothing to do with her. It was all to do with poor Duncan and forgiveness. Thinking of forgiveness, during the last hymn, as the coffin was carried out of the church, she glanced over at Peter. On the way up to the little village outside Sherborne, they hadn't said much and Kaisa wondered how Peter was feeling. She guessed he might have changed his mind about going to the funeral.

When the mourners started to make their way out of the church, Kaisa whispered into Peter's ear. 'Rose said there would be food and drinks at the pub opposite. What do you think?'

Peter moved his head away from Kaisa and lifted his dark eyes towards her. 'Don't think that's appropriate, do you?'

'No,' Kaisa said and lowered her head. They waited until the church was almost empty before making their way to the car, which was parked outside the village shop. As soon as Peter pulled onto the main road, the heavens opened and a sheet of rain hit the road in front of them. Large drops of water bounced off the bonnet of the car and the tarmac, making it difficult to see through the windscreen. Peter flicked the wipers on full and switched the headlights on, but it was no use.

'Pull over there,' Kaisa said, seeing a lay-by ahead.

'Bloody hell,' Peter said as he turned off the engine and

they heard the sound of the rain pound like machine-gun fire off the roof of the car.

Kaisa turned on her seat and placed a hand on Peter's knee. 'Thank you for coming today. I know it was difficult.'

'Not the most enjoyable day of my life, that's true,' Peter replied, placing his hand on top of Kaisa's. 'But I'm glad we came.' He leaned over and kissed Kaisa on the mouth.

The rain stopped as suddenly as it had started and Peter pulled back onto the road. After a few moments they could see a rainbow in the distance. Kaisa looked at the profile of her husband, and thought how lucky she was. Then she thought about Ravi, who hadn't called since they'd had their fight, if that's what it could be called.

'Peter,' she began, while he was waiting to enter a roundabout leading to the M3.

'Yes, my Peanut, what is it?' He glanced quickly at Kaisa, and then turned his attention to the traffic again.

Kaisa waited until they were cruising along the motorway.

'Ravi told me something the other day.'

'Oh, yes?' Peter said absentmindedly. He was now fiddling with the radio, trying to find a music station.

'He's gay.'

'Bloody hell!'

'Yeah, I know. I told him about Duncan and he got all funny and then just said, "Kaisa, I'm gay." Just like that.'

'When was this?'

Kaisa bit her lip. She hadn't thought this through.

Peter glanced at her again, this time his eyes had turned dark. 'You told him before you told me, didn't you?'

Kaisa was looking out of the window. The rain had left the road wet, with spray making it look slippery and danger-ous. 'Slow down, you're doing nearly 90!' she said.

'Don't change the subject,' Peter said but brought the speed down to nearer 70 miles per hour.

'OK, I did tell him before you, but only by a few weeks.'

'It doesn't matter if it was an hour before! I can't believe you. I thought we'd agreed: no more secrets!'

Kaisa felt close to tears, but tried to keep hold of herself.

'I was so lonely, and I had to tell someone. I didn't want to breathe a word of it at work, naturally, not something you'd talk about there, but when Ravi came over to the house, out of the blue, one evening, well I just couldn't ...'

Kaisa saw how Peter's mouth was in a straight line and he was staring at the road ahead. He put the indicator on and pulled out into the middle lane, overtaking a string of three cars. Spray formed in front of them and for an awful moment they couldn't see out of the windscreen, until the wipers began their sweeping motion across the glass. Again Kaisa noticed Peter was speeding, but she didn't dare say anything. He was taking out his anger on the road, and she hoped to God he'd calm down soon.

They spent the rest of the journey in silence, apart from when Kaisa asked Peter if he wanted to stop off for fish and chips as they got close to home. Peter nodded and soon they were parking the car a few steps away from their front door, carrying the delicious-smelling bag inside.

Kaisa arranged the food on plates and looked at Peter across the kitchen table. 'Look, darling, I didn't do it to spite you, or hurt you. You know I get lonely when you are away. Plus I didn't want to tell you all of this when I knew you needed to concentrate on Perisher.'

Peter lifted his head and sighed. 'I know.'

Kaisa walked around the table and went to hug her husband. 'I love you.'

Peter stroked Kaisa's hair, 'I know and I love you too. I think I'm a bit more stressed about the course than I realise.'

Kaisa pressed herself closer to Peter, nuzzling his neck. 'We'd better eat before it gets cold,' Kaisa said, but Peter had bent down and was kissing Kaisa. She could feel herself melt in his arms and desire rise inside her.

'Let's go upstairs,' Peter said hoarsely and almost carried Kaisa up the bedroom.

He peeled Kaisa's clothes off and pulled her knickers off, kneeling in front of her. Kaisa sighed and before she knew it, Peter was holding her legs and entering her, his eyes fixed on hers.

'You make me wild with desire, Kaisa,' he said and bent down to kiss her neck, breasts and mouth.

BEFORE PETER LEFT the house late on Sunday, they kissed and hugged for a long time. Kaisa was sad to be saying goodbye to him, she'd never get used to it, but it wasn't as bad as when he was about to go on a long patrol.

'I'll get a weekend off again soon,' Peter said, and brushed a strand of hair that had escaped from the ponytail Kaisa had fashioned, out of her face.

Kaisa smiled, 'Be careful, I might just get used to having you around.'

'Wouldn't that be something,' Peter replied. 'But honestly, I know I shouldn't say it, but I do have a good feeling about the future.' He placed his hand on Kaisa's belly.

Kaisa glanced down at his hand, then at Peter's face. 'Oh, darling, don't jinx it.'

Peter gave Kaisa a peck on her cheek and whispered into her ear, 'We've certainly given it a go this weekend.

What you did to me this morning, I'm getting hard just thinking about it.'

Kaisa blushed, she'd still not got used to talking openly about what they did in the privacy of their bedroom.

When Peter saw her face reddening, he squeezed her tightly against himself. 'Oh, darling, there's no need to be embarrassed. I love when you're passionate like that. Or didn't you notice?'

'Don't tease me,' Kaisa laughed, trying to shake off her discomfort. She knew it was silly, but she guessed it was the Finn in her. At home, you didn't talk about sex openly, if at all.

IN BED THAT NIGHT, Kaisa thought that everything was at last going right. Peter's words had echoed what she herself felt. She also had a good feeling about the future. She wondered if there was a little baby growing inside of her already, but immediately decided to cast such thoughts aside. She didn't want to put an adverse spell on any future pregnancy either.

TWENTY-ONE

'Well, well, Mrs Williams, it is indeed good news. Congratulations!'

Kaisa gazed at her doctor. His grey wisps of hair were a little longer today, showing off his unusually pale eyes. Kaisa wondered absentmindedly if they'd been blue when he was younger.

'Thank you, Dr Harris,' Kaisa replied and smiled. She'd been smiling to herself for weeks now. Although it was good to have the confirmation from her GP, she'd known before she came into the surgery that she was pregnant. This was the fourth time, so by now she recognised the signs. Exactly ten days after Peter had returned to the base and his Perisher course, Kaisa had gone off coffee. Then, she'd had the familiar metallic taste in her mouth, and a few days later, the final confirmation when she couldn't face breakfast in the morning. Her breasts had been sore right after Peter had gone, but she had thought that might have been because of all the sex they'd had. They'd made love several times a day over the weekend. It was as if the closeness of death had made them want to confirm that they were alive. Besides, she'd had an ulterior motive, which she was sure Peter knew was the reason she kept pulling him – very willingly – into bed. After all they'd discussed, after all the lies she'd confessed to, Peter still looked happier than she'd seen him in a long while when he said goodbye to her on the steps of their home.

Kaisa had taken a pregnancy test as soon as her period was a day late, and the little blue line had been clear on the stick. But she tried not to think about it until she had confirmation from her GP. Still, she couldn't help the utter feeling of happiness and fulfilment she had. She tried to keep fear out of her mind too, and for some reason, she was succeeding in not thinking the worst.

'So, because of your, hmm, history,' the doctor glanced at Kaisa's face, probably expecting her to dissolve into a flood of tears any moment. When he saw Kaisa smiling, he continued, visibly relieved, 'Yes, as I was saying, because of your recent terminations, we are able to offer you a course of treatment to ensure a successful pregnancy, hopefully right up to full term.'

'Oh,' Kaisa said. She'd heard from Pammy, her friend on the naval base in Faslane who had also suffered several miscarriages, that after three 'terminations' as the GP called her miscarriages, the NHS would offer some treatment or other. But she had no idea this treatment was offered automatically, or that is was something old Dr Harris would even know about. She assumed this time they'd just monitor her more closely.

'What do you mean by 'treatment' exactly?'

'Hormones,' the GP said. 'This is quite a new thing, but since you've terminated around the same time each pregnancy, I think it may be caused by a dip in your progesterone level and we can address that.' The man was looking at a brown folder, and not at Kaisa.

Kaisa stared at the doctor. Had he known the reason for the miscarriages all along? At first, she'd been convinced it was the nuclear reactor Peter worked so close to, or the AIDS virus. Almost every waking hour of the past few months, nearly a year, she'd wondered what the reason for her inability to keep hold of a baby could be. And here her doctor was, looking at the answer in her notes.

When there was no reaction from his patient, Dr Harris looked up at Kaisa. 'So we have two options. Either you will proceed with this pregnancy without our intervention and hope for the best, or we begin the treatment immediately.'

'What ... what is the treatment?' Kaisa said, stammering a little. She couldn't take in the news that there was a simple fix for her inability to keep hold of a baby. Just like that! She wished Peter was there with her. She wanted him to hold her hand now and ask sensible questions. In Kaisa's mind, only anger whirled, making her unable to utter a word. How could she ask her old GP why, if he'd already diagnosed the problem she had with losing babies, hadn't he told her before? Without coming across rude. The nights she'd spent wondering why her body had rejected the foetus, while all along this man had known the reason!

She looked out of the bay window of the surgery and saw normal people walking outside, doing their usual, everyday things. She noticed for the first time that the wide, beige-coloured vertical blinds, which were half open, looked shabby and faded. She was jolted back into the room when her GP spoke.

'Right, Mrs Williams, it is a 20-week course of injections. You will need to come to the surgery once a week. A nurse will administer the injection.' Dr Harris leaned forward on his chair and looked in Kaisa's eyes. 'This is a new treatment, and we cannot be sure that it works for each patient.'

Kaisa nodded, although she had a feeling that she wasn't in the room, but floating above it. She put her hands down on the chair, making sure she was sitting down properly, and took a couple of deep breaths in and out.

'Are you alright, Mrs Williams?' The GP's expression was full of concern.

'Could I have a glass of water?'

'Of course.' The old GP got to his feet and poured a glassful from a carafe on his desk. He watched as Kaisa sipped the water and placed the glass back onto the leather-covered surface.

Kaisa blinked and said, 'Yes, I understand. Injections once a week?'

'Is that OK?'

Suddenly Kaisa thought of something, 'I work shifts at the BBC. Does it have to be a certain day of the week?'

Dr Harris gazed at Kaisa. He tilted his head slightly and said, 'If you like we can leave your pregnancy to develop naturally, and, if you lose the baby again, try it next time?'

'No, let's do it now,' Kaisa said firmly and tried to smile. She was finally beginning to feel herself again.

'Excellent, I think that is a good decision. And I'm afraid you will have to have it the same day each week. But I'm sure your employer will understand?'

Kaisa nodded.

'Can I ask you something, Dr Harris?' Kaisa said after the doctor had told her to go back to the reception and wait for the nurse to call her.

'Of course, what is it?'

'Did you know all along that it was this hormone, pro ...'

Kaisa struggled with the pronunciation. 'Did you know the lack of it was the reason for all the previous miscarriages?'

Dr Harris hesitated, 'No, not really. I have a colleague, Dr Chishty, who advised me that this may be the problem. She is specialising in women's medicine and has been studying the cause of early miscarriages.'

'I see,' Kaisa said. She stood facing Dr Harris, her hand on the door handle.

'So you're lucky we have Dr Chishty at our disposal here,' Dr Harris said and smiled. Then, becoming serious, he added, 'But don't forget, there's no guarantee that it will work.'

TWENTY-TWO

Peter was snoozing in his bunk, trying to catch a few zzz's before he was due to have his session with Teacher in the control room, when Nigel came into the wardroom and nudged his shoulder.

'Ethan's off.'

'What?' Peter got up quickly and saw the Canadian standing in the gangway. His shoulders were slumped and he was looking down at his cap, which he held in one hand. Tony was next to him, patting his shoulder.

'Sorry, to see you go, mate,' he said and Peter could hear the genuine feeling in the throaty way his words came out. He realised how close they all had grown during the past couple of months. At that moment, Peter felt he almost liked the loud Australian.

When Peter and Nigel shook Ethan's hand, he could see the man's eyes look watery, and for a moment he wondered if he was going to cry. Then they saw Teacher's steward behind Ethan, carrying his canvas holdall. 'This way, Sir,' he said, nodding to the remaining Perishers to get out of their way. He ushered Ethan towards the conning tower.

Ethan's failure after only three days at sea came as a huge blow to all the other Perishers. All three remaining officers crowded into the small wardroom and sat in silence around the central table. They heard James Bond running empty alongside, but no one commented on its sudden appearance.

Eventually, Tony spoke up. 'He made another mash of his calculations this evening. Teacher had to take charge of the sub, and that was one time too many.'

It seemed the older man hadn't been able to keep up with the mental arithmetic.

Peter shook his head at Tony, but said nothing.

'I'll miss him,' Nigel said, and then added, 'but that's the name of the game, eh, chaps?'

Peter and Tony nodded.

A senior rating popped his head through the door, and addressing Peter said, 'Sir, you are required in the control room.'

'Thank you, I'll be right there.'

Peter got up and fetched his stop-watch from his bunk and put it around his neck. He took a deep breath and focused on what he needed to do. He had to concentrate on the forthcoming exercises and forget about Ethan and his departure. For one thing, it meant that if the statistics were anything to go by, the three remaining Perishers were safe. Wasn't it one in four that generally failed? Peter shook his head; he mustn't think that either. Teacher had made it very clear to them that every Perisher could fail. What mattered was that those who passed had both the aptitude and the leadership skills, as well as the technical ability to captain one of Her Majesty's submarines. If there was any doubt in Teacher's mind that something was amiss with any of them, they'd be escorted off. If the Perisher couldn't ignore jibes about a past event in a naval base pool with a fellow officer, for example. Or jokes about the honour of the candidate's wife.

Peter wondered if Duncan's death had filtered through to the crew. What would they say if they knew he'd attended the funeral? Peter hadn't spotted anyone else from Duncan's Navy days at the church; but he couldn't be sure he'd know everyone anyway.

He'd penned a short letter to Jeff, his best man, who had been at Dartmouth with him and Duncan, but he knew Jeff was in the Falkland Islands and wouldn't be home for months. Peter shuddered and told himself to stop thinking about anything else but what he had been taught. *Concentrate, man!*

After the weekend at home, even after spending Saturday brooding over the sorry affair of his former friend, he'd felt in excellent spirits on his return to the submarine, full of confidence that he'd finish the two weeks sea-time with flying colours.

No one had mentioned his past, or Duncan, and even the Aussie had kept his mouth shut on that score. Peter had told both Ethan and Tony about the sudden death, not mentioning AIDS out of courtesy to his former mate. Both had been quiet, and Peter had suspected they'd already heard through the grapevine. As well as Ethan, Peter had grown quite fond of Tony. It seemed that the incident in the pub in Brodick was all forgotten.

But the sea-time was challenging. The scenarios Teacher put the Perishers through were more complicated than Peter had imagined. At yesterday's exercise he'd had three frigates coming at the boat at once, and it had got very close to Teacher taking control of the submarine. That had happened to Peter only once towards the end of the first sea-time trials, but he knew that if it happened again, he'd be a gonner. Just like Ethan.

TWENTY-THREE

Kaisa had decided not to tell Peter about her pregnancy until after he'd finished Perisher. Whether he passed or failed, he needed to concentrate on the course without worrying about Kaisa or thinking about a baby. The Duncan affair was distraction enough; he didn't need any more dramas.

The wonderful thing was that Peter was able to telephone her almost every week, and the night before her appointment with Dr Harris, when Peter was on his way out to join the sub, he'd sounded buoyant on the phone. 'It's all going well, just the two weeks at sea and I will be able to come home.'

The week the doctor had confirmed her pregnancy and offered Kaisa the hormone injections, Peter had begun the second, and the final, sea-time.

It was now mid-September and the evenings were getting cooler and the weather worsening. Kaisa had been sitting on the bottom step of the staircase at Chepstow Place, watching the rain beat against the living room windows. She'd come so close to telling Peter the happy news during their conversations. But she'd kept her head, and it was now only a matter of weeks before he'd be done. Or be hoisted off the submarine. It was harsh punishment for failure, but Peter had explained to Kaisa that it was a necessary rule. 'You don't want a bitter, old, failed Perisher breathing down a captain's neck in the control room.' Of course, neither of them had mentioned the possibility of failure since it would only bring bad luck.

But when the phone rang in the hall early on the morning of 30th September, and Kaisa's bum was still smarting from the injection that she'd had the day before, she had resolved to tell Peter about the baby. She was ten weeks gone now; four weeks further in the pregnancy than she'd ever been before, and she was already beginning to show. She needed to talk to Peter about what to tell people at work. She also wanted to tell her mum and sister, and Ravi, if he ever spoke to her again, as well as Rose.

But not before Peter knew.

Kaisa lifted the receiver and said, 'Hello?' even though she expected it would be Peter at six am on a Sunday. (Although her mother had been known to call early at the weekend too.)

'I'm coming home,' Peter said. His voice was thin and he sounded tense.

The first thought Kaisa had was where she should hide the bottle of champagne she'd bought at Marks & Spencer on Oxford Street the previous day. She had stood in the store, staring at the wine display, and eventually picked up a bottle. Even if Peter failed Perisher, she thought, they could still celebrate the baby, although the prospect of an alcoholic drink made her feel a bit queasy. Now, though, she realised how stupid the purchase had been.

'OK,' she said.

'I'm going to be home late afternoon,' Peter continued in the same serious voice.

'Are you OK, Peter?' Kaisa asked.

There was a silence at the other end.

'Peter?' Kaisa said. She was getting worried now.

'Not really.'

Oh, Peter, I'm so sorry.'

Again Peter was silent.

'Let me know what flight and I'll come and meet you at Heathrow.'

'No need. I'm not sure of the timings yet.'

'OK,' Kaisa said.

'Will you be home?'

'Of course,' Kaisa said. She put her right hand on her extended tummy. She was wearing Peter's old white uniform shirt and his thick submarine socks. She liked to sleep in something that even after several washes smelt faintly of Peter. And the house was permanently cold, so to save on heating bills when the weather got cooler, she wore the woolly socks too.

'Peter, do you know if you passed yet?' Kaisa said while holding tightly onto the receiver.

'No, I don't.'

'But what do you think?'

'Oh Kaisa, I don't know, darling. But it doesn't matter, really, does it?'

Suddenly Kaisa could hear the warmth in Peter's voice. 'I love you,' she said.

'Same,' Peter said. Kaisa knew he was smiling by the way he sounded, and she knew he would have told her he loved he if he could. There were probably several people listening in on their conversation.

'I've got to go, darling,' Peter said, 'I'll be home soon.'

But Kaisa couldn't wait. 'Peter, don't go yet. I have something to tell you.'

'Really?' Again Kaisa could hear the smile in his voice.

'Yes, I'm 10 weeks.'

Kaisa could hear Peter catch his breath, 'That's wonderful news!'

'And, Dr Harris is giving me this new treatment; hormone injections for 20 weeks. They are hopeful that it'll sort out the problem.'

'Kaisa, you've made me the happiest man alive.'

Kaisa swallowed hard. She wanted to cry out of joy. Peter was happy; even if he had failed Perisher, he was still over the moon that he would finally become a father. She hugged the receiver even closer to her ear, as if she was holding onto Peter.

'Hurry home,' she whispered.

'I will,' Peter said and he was gone.

Kaisa sat on the steps for a few minutes more, holding onto the receiver, listening to the empty tone at the other end of the line. *I've made him the happiest man alive.*

TWENTY-FOUR

They'd carried out their final exercises. They'd all been allowed to phone their wives, or family, to say they'd be home that evening. The three men sat in the small wardroom and waited. They knew Teacher would call the three remaining Perishers, one by one, into the Captain's cabin.

Nigel was the first to be summoned by the Coxswain. Tony and Peter didn't speak while they waited. Both were tired from the most challenging days at sea they'd ever faced, and nervous about their fate. No words were needed now; each knew exactly how the other felt.

Peter gazed down at his hands and thought about Kaisa and their future together. He allowed himself to dream about holding his son or daughter in his arms, a small round-bellied thing, smiling up at him. He would be a father after all. He thought about the close call they'd had with AIDS, about Duncan's passing and about the treatment Kaisa was receiving. He knew she'd never gone as far as she was now. His heart was filled with trepidation at the prospect of perhaps having to start a new career just as he was becoming a father. Would he be able to provide for his family if he failed Perisher and decided to leave the Navy? He knew he didn't have to, there would be jobs and possibly a perfectly satisfactory career ahead of him in surface ships, but would he want to stay if he could no longer serve in submarines? His naval career would be marred by two black spots: a Court Martial for striking a now deceased fellow officer, and a failed Perisher course.

Suddenly Nigel stood in the gangway, grinning from ear to ear. The Coxswain was standing next to him, addressing Tony, 'Your turn, Sir.'

'Well done, mate,' Tony said, getting up and shaking Nigel's hand. 'Here goes, wish me luck, boys,' he added, placing his cap on his head, leaving Peter and Nigel behind in the cramped wardroom.

'Congratulations, I knew you'd do it,' Peter said and hugged his friend.

Nigel sat down and leaned back on the wardroom sofa, which also served as his bed. He put his hands over his head and exhaled deeply, letting air out of his lungs. With a wide grin he said, 'Thank you. It feels good!' Then, remembering that Peter had not yet found out his fate, he added, 'You'll be OK.'

Peter looked at his old friend. He wasn't at all sure he'd passed. But he couldn't help but smile.

'Kaisa is pregnant again,' he said.

'That's great news. Congratulations!'

Peter was too nervous to tell his friend about the treatment Kaisa was getting; besides, he knew Nigel wouldn't be able to concentrate on Peter and Kaisa's problems. He'd passed Perisher and Peter was glad for his friend. Would he follow in Nigel's footsteps?

The last three weeks at sea had been taxing, and he

knew he wasn't as good technically as his friend, and he also lacked the ability to think as quickly as the Aussie did. Although Tony was sometimes a bit too flamboyant, and could fly off the handle at the crew, a side to him that Peter knew too well, he also knew that it had not been a problem during the last – critical – weeks of the Perisher course. Somehow Tony had been able to control his temper. So he'd probably pass as well.

Which left Peter.

Was it a bad sign that he was the last one to be called into Teacher's cabin?

EVERYTHING AFTER PETER's meetings with Teacher was a bit of a blur.

When he'd stepped back into the wardroom and Peter had told the others what the Teacher had said, Tony had got a bottle of Scotch from the small cabinet serving as a bar in the corner of the wardroom and poured them all a large drink.

'It's over boys!' Nigel had said, and they'd all downed the strong liquid in large gulps, while waiting for Teacher's steward to pack their bags. It was the tradition that when the Perishers left the training boat for the last time, the practical things would be handled for them.

'You flying down South straight away?' Nigel asked Peter, and he nodded. He seemed to have lost his ability to speak. Kaisa's news and the meeting with Teacher had made him feel shaky. He leaned against the bulkhead and tried to steady himself. It must be the alcohol that had gone straight to his head.

When, a few minutes later, the three of them were escorted off the submarine, Peter still felt unsteady as he climbed up the conning tower. Outside, the cold, fresh air hit his face and filled his nostrils. He put on his cap and felt a little better. He even allowed himself a slight smile. He'd soon have Kaisa, a pregnant Kaisa, in his arms.

He walked along the casing and noticed it was slippery. He was the last one off the submarine, and saw Tony and Nigel had already climbed onboard James Bond.

It was a dark night. Little wind, no stars, just a faint light in distance marking the horizon. Peter wondered what time it was, and realised he had no idea if the silvery light was fading into night or an indication of the sun coming up. He hadn't recognised he'd stopped walking, gawking at the view, until he heard Teacher's steward, who was behind him, carrying Peter's bag say, 'It's cold, let's get onboard, Sir.' His hand stretched out in front of Peter, guiding him towards the waiting launch.

Peter moved forward towards the vessel. The two-man crew onboard saluted him, and he in turn saluted Teacher, making an effort to stand erect on the casing. The man, who Peter suddenly saw looked weary, nodded, took his hand and said simply, 'Captain.'

Peter replied, 'Sir,' and proceeded to get onboard James Bond. He smiled, turned and stepped out, but somehow his foot missed the edge of the other vessel, and at the same time his back leg slipped on the casing of the submarine. He heard the voices of people shouting, while his brain registered the harsh chill in every part of his body, except his head.

He was in the water, and it was cold. He felt the dampness creep into his clothes and hit his skin. His legs felt heavy, so heavy that they were dragging him under. He thrashed madly with his arms, trying to get hold of something, but the side of the submarine was further away, and the hull of James Bond, bobbing on the water, grew more and more distant.

Suddenly, he realised what was dragging him further away – the propeller. He made an effort to calm himself and began fighting the drag with his legs, pounding the water hard, and for a moment, he thought he was making headway.

All I need to do is keep going and they'll get me out of the water.

Images of Kaisa smiling, holding a baby in her arms, came into his mind, as he felt himself being dragged under.

No, this can't be it, not now. Not now when everything is so good.

His head bobbed underneath the surface of the freezing water, filling his mouth and lungs with cold water. He fought against the strong pull of the sea, sucking him further down, and got his face up. He gulped in air. He could see a flashing light coming from somewhere, but a second later his lungs filled with water again and blackness overtook him.

TWENTY-FIVE

After Kaisa had spoken with Peter, she phoned the newsroom at the BBC and told them to leave a message with the duty editor to say that she was too ill to come into work. She told them she had a tummy bug. She climbed back into bed for an hour, trying to sleep. But she couldn't stop thinking about how wonderful Peter had sounded and how he said she'd made him the happiest man alive. Although she knew that he felt the same way about the baby as she did, it was such a relief to hear him say that the foetus growing inside her was more important to him than his career. Or whether he passed Perisher or not.

Kaisa put her hands across her belly and closed her eyes. She wanted to rest so that she'd look fresh when Peter arrived home later that day. She thought about how he'd touch her tummy, and kiss her lips and gently hold her close.

None of her pregnancies before had gone far enough for him to see a visible bump. At only six weeks each time, she hadn't really felt there was a real baby there, apart from perhaps the first time, when they hadn't realised how easily a baby could be lost.

Kaisa thought back to last year, when she had fallen pregnant for the first time. How joyous and carefree she had felt about it then! They had later realised the baby had been conceived in France during their summer holiday with Ravi.

That autumn, Peter had been serving in a diesel submarine, which was on a refit in Plymouth, so he'd been home every weekend. When, after they had returned home, her period had been a week late, she'd suspected something was up and bought a pregnancy test at the Boots on Kensington High Street. It was a Wednesday, and she'd wanted to wait until Peter was home for the weekend, but in the end she had peed on the stick the very next morning. She had hardly believed her eyes when the blue line appeared. The same day she'd gone and bought another test and got the same result the next morning.

When she told Peter about the baby over the phone the next evening, he'd been pleased, but not as emotional as he had sounded this morning. Now they both knew how easily this one too could be lost.

As Kaisa nodded off, she smiled to herself. For some reason, whether it was to do with the hormone treatment she was having, or Peter's warm voice still ringing in her ears, she had a feeling that this little baby would stick around.

It was late afternoon when Kaisa saw a naval padre, followed by a naval officer she didn't know, standing by her door.

Kaisa was on her way home, carrying her shopping bags

out of the car. Although feeling guilty about calling in sick at work, and nervous about bumping into someone she knew, Kaisa had gone into town and bought two steaks and ready-made Dauphinoise potatoes, which she knew Peter particularly loved, from Marks & Spencer. She also got herself a new dress; a loose powder-blue A-line thing that she knew would do her for a few months before the bump became too large for anything but proper maternity wear.

Even though she didn't want to think about it, she'd bought the dress because she'd be able to wear it even when she wasn't pregnant. After the baby, she told herself, feigning a confidence she didn't have. She'd decided she would be positive about this pregnancy. She'd heard somewhere – perhaps it was Rose who had told her – that positive thinking could beat breast cancer. Why wouldn't it help her hold onto this baby she was carrying? She would try everything in her power to hold onto it, even if it meant going all 'New Age' on Peter. She laughed at the thought of Peter on a vegetarian camp somewhere, wearing a colourful kaftan and practising yoga with her.

She didn't notice the two men standing in her front garden until she was passing her neighbour's house. She spotted their backs, as they stood outside her door, ringing the bell. Then the padre turned around, and seeing her standing there, watching them, he said something to the officer next to him. The unknown man was in a uniform, much like Peter's, except that he had thin hair, which she saw when he took off his naval cap. Both men began to walk towards her. Realising she had stopped, she started to make her way down the path.

'Mrs Williams?'

'Yes,' Kaisa said, moving her shopping from her right

hand to her left and rummaging in her handbag for the house keys. 'I'm afraid my husband isn't home,' she said.

The two men exchanged looks, and again the older officer spoke, 'Can we go inside, please, Mrs Williams?'

Kaisa nodded, 'Yes, but as I said, Peter isn't at home yet, so ...' she said, finally bringing out the keys. The man interrupted her, 'I am Lieutenant Commander Stephen Crowther and this is Mr William Davies.'

'How do you do,' Kaisa said and shifted her shopping to the crook of her arm. It was heavier than she had realised it would be when she filled her trolley at Marks & Spencer.

'Can I take that and carry it for you?' Lieutenant Commander Stephen Crowther said, and without waiting for her reply he picked up the carrier bags. Kaisa nodded, and while the men took her shopping, she opened the door and ushered the two of them inside.

'Would you like a cup of tea?' she asked as soon as they were in the small hall. As she showed Lieutenant Commander Crowther and Mr Davies into their front room, she let out a sigh of relief that she'd cleaned the house before going into town. But the men wouldn't sit; instead they stood in the room, filling it with their presence and making it look cramped and tiny.

'No thank you,' they both said in unison. Then, exchanging glances once more, the older of the two, Crowther, spoke.

'Mrs Williams, why don't you take a seat.'

Kaisa stared at the men, and realising they wouldn't sit unless she herself did, she smoothed down her cotton skirt and seated herself on the blue sofa, the first item of furniture she and Peter had bought when they moved in.

The two men immediately sat down opposite her on the white sofa that Peter and Kaisa had found in Habitat last summer. They'd bought it after Kaisa had lost her first baby, when she'd told Peter that she wouldn't want to try again. The sofa was terribly impractical, and showed every little stain, but at the time it had seemed the perfect buy for a childless couple.

'Mrs Williams, I'm afraid we have some bad news.' Lieutenant Commander Crowther was the first to speak again. He seemed to be in the lead, but even he looked nervous and unsure of himself. Kaisa couldn't think why they would bring a naval Padre along to tell Peter that he'd failed Perisher. If that was what this charade was all about.

'I'm sorry, I don't understand,' Kaisa said. 'My husband, Lieutenant Commander Williams isn't here, so ...'

'It's Lieutenant Commander Williams, Peter, we are here to speak to you about.' Crowther was fiddling with his naval cap.

'Oh?'

The Padre got up and came to sit next to Kaisa. 'Mrs Williams, may I call you Kaisa?'

Kaisa looked at the Padre with suspicion. The last time she'd had a Padre sit next to her on a sofa was when he had told her he couldn't provide Peter with the correct documentation to marry her in Finland. That had resulted in a quickie marriage in the registry office in Portsmouth and a blessing in Finland instead of the full-blown wedding ceremony everyone had been expecting.

She couldn't understand what was going on now. Unless ... fear crept up her spine and circled her tummy. She felt her mouth go dry. She nodded to the Padre.

'I'm sorry to tell you, Mrs Williams, Kaisa, that your husband, Peter, had an accident onboard the submarine early this morning.' It was the officer, Crowther, speaking across from Kaisa.

'An accident?' Kaisa heard herself say. Her voice sounded as if it was coming from a deep well, and not from her own mouth at all. She felt the room and Crowther and the Padre, whose name she had suddenly forgotten, grow more and more distant, as if she was moving backwards into a tunnel.

'Yes, an accident.' The man opposite her, or the Padre, Kaisa wasn't sure which one of the faraway figures was speaking, said, 'It was a terrible accident. Peter slipped on the casing when he was about to step onboard the transport vessel and he fell overboard.'

'Is he OK? Where is he?' Kaisa said. Her speech, as well as her vision, seemed to have worsened. She could hardly get the words out. She got up, knowing she had to go to Peter. She had to see how he was. But she felt dizzy and began swaying.

Kaisa felt the hands of the man on her. Or perhaps it was the Padre with his black clothes who was holding her and pulling her back to the seat?

'Mrs Williams, you must keep calm.'

Kaisa nodded. Then she heard a noise and realised it was coming from her. She put her hand on her mouth. *You must keep calm. They won't tell you anything unless you keep calm.* Kaisa nodded and lifted her eyes to the man opposite her.

'I'm so sorry, so terribly sorry to tell you this, but your husband's accident was fatal.'

There was a silence.

'You mean, he's ..., what do you mean, *fatal?*' Kaisa said. She was still holding onto her mouth, and felt wet tears fall onto her fingers. She couldn't breathe.

Now one of the men was crouching in front of her,

touching her shoulder, 'Yes I am so terribly sorry but Lieutenant Commander Williams, Peter, your husband is dead.'

Suddenly the room began spinning in front of Kaisa's eyes, and everything went so bright she had to close her eyes.

TWENTY-SIX

Pirjo booked the next available flight and turned up at the house in Chepstow Place the day after Peter's death. Her eyes looked swollen and blood-shot and she hugged Kaisa hard.

'How did you know?' Kaisa said when at last she settled down with a cup of coffee Ravi had brewed for them. Pirjo gave Kaisa's Indian friend a long stare, but with his usual charm, Ravi soon won her mother over.

After the Padre and the naval officer had managed to wake Kaisa up after she'd fainted in front of the two men in her own living room, they'd asked if there was anyone, any family, Kaisa could call. The only person, apart from Rose, who Kaisa didn't want to call on so soon after Duncan's passing, was Ravi.

'He's gone,' was all Kaisa could say down the phone when she'd called his office. He'd hurried to the house on Chepstow Place and hadn't left Kaisa's side for 48 hours.

Now Pirjo, sitting opposite her daughter at the pine table, lowered her voice. 'I'm here now so you don't need anyone else.'

Kaisa hadn't had the energy to argue. 'I'm pregnant,' she said instead.

Kaisa's mother stared at her daughter and squeezed her hands even tighter.

'I'm having hormone injections, which the doctor thinks will stop me from losing this one.'

Pirjo nodded. 'Oh my darling girl.' Tears ran down her face again and Kaisa had to look away. She couldn't cope with her mother's grief. Besides, what did she have to be sorry about? *It wasn't her husband who had died, she hadn't lost anyone.* Kaisa was hit by a surge of anger so strong that she had to get up.

'I'm tired,' she said and went up to the bedroom.

Upstairs she hit a pillow, and threw it against the built-in wardrobe that stood at the foot of the bed. The thin panel shook for a while, but didn't have the decency to break, so she threw a pregnancy book she'd got from WH Smith's. Again, the veneer panel vibrated slightly, which made Kaisa even angrier. She took hold of the glass of water she always kept on the bedside table and hurled it at the wardrobe. Water and glass flew in all directions, and for a moment Kaisa felt good, but when the door opened and her mother walked in, with Ravi close behind her, and she saw them staring at her, and at the mess on the carpet, she felt ashamed. She sat down on the floor and blacked out.

Kaisa woke later, fully clothed on top of her bed. Someone had placed a crocheted blanket over her legs. She opened her eyes and sat up in bed. She felt her tummy and smiled, because she'd forgotten. For a few delicious seconds, she was happy about the baby, looking forward to seeing Peter later; wasn't he supposed to be at home already?

And then she remembered.

Slowly the faces of the naval commander and the padre

came into focus, the strangers who had come with the most horrible news, and she recalled the words: *I am so terribly sorry but Lieutenant Commander Williams, Peter, your husband, is dead.* Kaisa put her head into her hands and began howling. She wrapped her hands around her body and began rocking back and forth.

'Kaisa, you must calm down,' her mother was by her side and holding down her hands, trying to stop her movement. But Kaisa couldn't stop; the only thing that helped at least a little was being able to move, to be able to shout and cry. When Kaisa brushed her mother away Ravi took her place. The man with the beautiful brown eyes crouched in front of her and said, 'Shh, shh, it's OK.' He put his arms around her and whispered in her ear, 'Think of the baby, Kaisa, think about the baby.'

The baby, the fatherless baby. Kaisa thought and carried on crying.

'You're frightening the baby,' Ravi said and Kaisa put her hands on her tummy. Somehow she'd managed to stop the rocking back and forth. And at that moment, she felt a movement, or not even movement, more like the wings of a butterfly fluttering inside her tummy. She looked up at Ravi and said, 'It kicked, the baby kicked!'

They all laughed; made stupid noises somewhere between weeping and whooping. Ravi and Pirjo put their hands on Kaisa's tummy. She didn't feel any more movements, but it was a sign, a sign for Kaisa.

After that, Kaisa's mother and Ravi agreed that he would leave Kaisa and Pirjo alone in the house and go back to his flat in Holland Park. He promised to check up on Kaisa each afternoon on his way back from work, just in case there was a repeat of her 'attack', she assumed.

During the two weeks Pirjo spent with Kaisa, she

cleaned the little house from top to bottom, and made Peter's parents welcome when they arrived two days later, fighting tears and hugging Kaisa hard.

On the third day after Peter's death, when dusk had settled over the house and garden, and they were sitting in the lounge, Peter's parents perching on the white sofa and her own mother sitting on the armrest of the comfy chair that Kaisa had chosen, she told them about the baby.

'I'm getting hormone injections, so this one should stick,' Kaisa added. She was again fighting tears, but it seemed there were none left. She was so very tired, so very tired of it all. The telephone had been going all day, with people wanting to speak to her. But she didn't have the strength to talk to anyone, so while she was trying to sleep upstairs, her mother, with her faltering English, had thanked them for their condolences and tried to explain that Kaisa would not be coming to the phone.

As the news of the baby sank in, Kaisa saw tears in Peter's father's eyes. He got up and touched her knee, saying, 'Well done.' Awkwardly, not knowing what else to do, he backed off and, looking at his wife for help, sat down on the sofa again.

In her turn, Peter's mother said, 'God is merciful,' and got up and kissed Kaisa on the cheek. Kaisa stared at the tall, lanky woman and thought, *No, God is cruel and evil*, but she didn't say anything.

TWENTY-SEVEN

The day of the funeral was a ridiculously sunny, early October morning. The beautiful little house in Notting Hill was swathed in autumn sunshine, as Kaisa, Pirjo, Ravi and Peter's parents all piled into the three black funeral cars.

Seeing the coffin inside the hearse, draped with the White Ensign, Kaisa's knees buckled and she took hold of the doorframe. Her mother was behind her and supported Kaisa as she walked towards the waiting car.

It was just ten days after the visit she'd had from the Padre and Lieutenant Commander Crowther. There were some high-ranking Navy officers, including Peter's best man Jeff, and Peter's former Captain, Stewart, smartly dressed in their gold-braided uniforms in spite of the IRA threat.

Kaisa thought absentmindedly that this must be a special occasion, like a royal wedding or something. She also saw Jeff's parents, looking old and frail next to Peter's friend. Kaisa forced herself to say a few words to all of them.

There were so many people at the funeral, some of whom Kaisa remembered from her days in Portsmouth and

Helensburgh. She nodded to those she could remember and tried to keep herself steady. She felt so shaky, as if her body didn't want to enter the Kensal Green Chapel they'd chosen for the funeral. She was grateful to Lieutenant Commander Crowther, or Stephen, as he'd insisted she should call him, who now came to stand by her side with Ravi and her mother. He gently guided them all through the day. He'd helped her so much, and had organised the funeral service with Peter's parents.

The only detail Kaisa had insisted on was that the ceremony would be held in London, close to her. She knew Peter wanted to be either buried at sea or cremated. She had insisted Stephen tell her exactly how Peter had died, but had fainted again when he'd told her he'd been caught up in the submarine's propeller. *He got his wish to be buried at sea*, Kaisa had thought later. The cremation would be a formality, as there would hardly be any ashes to put in the urn. Yet Kaisa wanted a place where she could visit Peter, so there was to be a stone.

As the funeral party made their way into the chapel, Stephen spotted a gaggle of newspaper photographers outside. He asked Kaisa if it would be okay for them to have a few pictures, and she nodded. He organised everyone to pose in front of the double doors, then asked the journalists politely but firmly to leave.

When the music started Kaisa sat in the chapel, staring at Peter's coffin, trying to comprehend what had happened and that he wasn't ever going to be in their little house in Chepstow Place ever again. She clutched the single red rose she was going to place on the gravestone, and Ravi held her other hand the whole of the time.

Beside her, Pirjo and Peter's mother sat and wept quietly. Peter's father stared ahead of him, sitting upright, holding his wife's hand. Peter's siblings and their partners sat in the next row. Kaisa had hugged his family briefly, unable to look at Nancy or Simon's sad faces for long. Rose and her husband Roger sat behind them, and afterwards they, along with Stephen and the rest of the family, came back to Chepstow Place, where Ravi had organised a buffet and drinks.

IN THE KITCHEN, Kaisa could hear the voices of people talking in hushed tones in the lounge. She knew she needed to get back to the guests, but her legs were numb, and she was unable to move. Shifting in her seat, she suddenly realised her tummy was touching the edge of the table. She looked down at the growing baby inside her and realised she had to cope, she needed to be sane and well for Peter's child. She got up from the table and, wiping the tears from her eyes, walked into the lounge.

Among all the people drinking wine and chatting and making the room seem tiny, the first person Kaisa spotted was her mother. She wanted to bury her face in Pirjo's embrace and ask the people to leave. But Pirjo took hold of her arm, supported her to an empty sofa, and sat down next to her daughter. With her mother's help, Kaisa managed to get through the day.

TWENTY-EIGHT

On the day before she was about to fly back to Helsinki, Pirjo asked Kaisa if they could go out for lunch. Kaisa didn't know if she was ready to face the world yet, but guessed this was some kind of test her mother had devised to see if she could leave her alone. So Kaisa nodded and chose a place nearby, The Earl of Lonsdale, which she knew served decent food. She'd been to The Earl many times with Peter, and with Rose, as well as Ravi, and had to steel herself when she walked inside. Of course, the landlord was about and gave Kaisa a nod. 'I was so sorry to hear about Peter.'

'Thank you,' Kaisa said. She'd forgotten that Peter's horrible accident had been in the papers. In one way that helped her, because she didn't have to tell people, but on the other Kaisa didn't want to share her grief with the world. There had been a couple of reporters ringing the doorbell asking for an interview. Kaisa had told Ravi and then Pirjo to tell them a simple 'No.' She couldn't face anyone, not talk about Peter with anyone.

'I'll have a Coke – and a glass of wine,' she now said to

the landlord, and she glanced at her mother. 'And the menu please.' The man nodded and went to get the drinks.

'I'll find us a table, can you bring them over?' Kaisa said to Pirjo, and her mother nodded.

She sat in the far corner of the pub, which was half full of lunchtime drinkers, some of them tourists studying their maps, and a few builders in paint-splattered overalls hugging their pints of beer. Kaisa turned her eyes away from a couple drinking a bottle of wine, who were sitting close to one another and smiling. She looked at her mother, who was speaking in hushed tones with the landlord and sighed with relief. With her little English, Pirjo had managed to talk to the man about Peter so Kaisa didn't have to. Now all Kaisa needed to do was avoid his gaze when he came to bring them the food.

When Pirjo came back with the drinks, she smiled. 'I'm going to be drunk on my plane home.'

She was changing the subject on purpose, Kaisa knew, and gratefully replied, 'No you won't.'

Kaisa would have been glad of the numbing effect of alcohol, but even if she'd allow herself to have a glass, which the midwife had said would be OK, she felt nauseous at just the thought of it.

After they'd chosen their meals and Kaisa had been back to the bar, taking her chance to order the food with a new barmaid she didn't recognise, Pirjo said, 'I wanted to talk to you, Kaisa, before I leave.'

'Oh yes?' Kaisa said.

They'd been doing nothing but talk all fortnight. After the first few days, when Peter's parents had been in the house, and then after the funeral, a day that was mostly a haze in Kaisa's mind, when all Kaisa wanted to do was sleep, Kaisa and Pirjo had been talking about everything.

Kaisa had told her how wonderful Peter had been on the phone, and how he'd said she'd made him the happiest man alive. She had poured her heart out to her mother, telling her about her regrets, speaking again about the awfulness of the first year of marriage and her unfaithfulness with Duncan, and her friendship with Rose, who had promised to come up to London when Pirjo had gone home. Of course, Pirjo knew all of it already, but it helped Kaisa to say it all again, to tell her mother how happy Peter had made her in spite of everything.

Pirjo had listened and had hugged Kaisa, even sleeping with her when Kaisa couldn't settle in the middle of the night.

'I want you to think about what you are going to do now.'

'What do you mean?'

'You need to think about your future. It's not easy to bring a child up on your own.'

'I know,' Kaisa said. She was looking at Pirjo's face trying to find out what she was talking about.

'Come back to Finland!'

'No!' Kaisa said, a little too loudly.

People around them looked up from their drinks. Even the love birds lifted their gaze and stared at Kaisa and Pirjo.

Pirjo put her hand on Kaisa's arm, 'All I'm saying is that you should think of yourself.'

Kaisa was silent for a while then said, quietly, 'I am thinking of myself.'

'And the baby? Do you think you will be able to give the baby a good life in England?'

'Yes!' Again Kaisa raised her voice, but when she saw the landlord put down a glass he was wiping, she lowered her voice and whispered to her mother, 'This is my home now. I was very happy here with Peter.' Kaisa swallowed hard. She couldn't' go on. She removed her hand from the table and from under her mother's grasp and placed both hands on her lap, looking down at them. *Keep calm, keep calm.*

Pirjo leaned back in her red velvet chair and sighed. 'All I wanted to do is make you understand that it'd be easier for you to be at home.'

Kaisa lifted her eyes to her mother's. 'The Navy is looking after me financially, and I have my job. And Ravi and Rose.'

It was Pirjo's time to be quiet. She looked down at her glass, then lifted her eyes up at Kaisa again. 'But are you sure? You're a foreigner here and always will be, won't you?'

Kaisa took a deep breath, and then another, in an attempt to calm down. She felt stronger now and had her eyes squarely on her mother. 'This is my home now. I will have this baby here, and he or she will be English, just like Peter. Our home and place is here.'

Pirjo nodded. 'OK, but just think about what I said.'

'Mum, I know you're thinking of me, but this baby I'm carrying is half English. He or she is part of Peter, and the only thing I have left of him now.' Tears were welling inside Kaisa, but she continued, 'and for now I can't think about moving anywhere.'

In the last few hours Kaisa spent with Pirjo, she tried not to show her frustration with her, and kept quiet. Of course, Pirjo noticed, and when they parted at Heathrow, her mother said, 'Don't think badly of me for what I said. I was only thinking of you. At least think about coming back home, eh?'

Kaisa had nodded and hugged her mother hard. She

was fighting tears again, and wondered if she had been right to dismiss moving back to Finland so hastily.

The day after Kaisa'a mother had returned to Finland, the telephone in the hall rang. It was just past 6 pm and Ravi and Kaisa were sitting in front of the TV in the lounge, watching the evening news.

'You expecting a call?' Ravi said.

Kaisa shook her head. They'd got into a routine during those few first weeks after Peter's passing: if the telephone went, Ravi, or her mother, would reply in case Kaisa wasn't up to talking to yet another Navy Wife who felt she needed to convey her and her husband's condolences.

Kaisa was surprised how little of this English etiquette she could take before she felt close to tears, so Ravi, bless his heart, had taken upon himself to listen to the same platitudes over and over. He was excellent at making excuses for Kaisa not being able to come to the telephone; she was asleep, in the bath (Kaisa never took baths; she preferred the shower), or at the shops. One time, Ravi even told someone that Kaisa had nipped out to buy milk for his tea, an excuse that particular Navy Wife (whom Kaisa couldn't even remember meeting) swallowed easily. Why wouldn't a woman take care of the man in the house – even a 'Paki friend' as Ravi put it when they laughed about the call almost a year later, when Kaisa found she could see the funny side to life again.

Kaisa knew she was being selfish and impolite, but she didn't care. She had pulled the short straw in life, and she didn't need to pander to anyone's sensibilities anymore. She couldn't care less what any Navy Wife – or anyone in the Navy for that matter – thought of her behaviour. If they didn't like it, they could try losing a husband in the senseless way she had. She bet they'd not care about being polite or doing things the right way either in the circumstances.

'It's your sister, I think?' Ravi now said, looking at Kaisa and holding onto the receiver.

'Hello Sirkka, you feeling any better?' Kaisa tried to put on a jolly voice for her sister.

Kaisa had spoken to Sirkka several times after Peter's death. They'd had long, long phone calls in which Kaisa had poured her heart out, and they had both cried and cried. Sirkka had been feeling too sick with her pregnancy to come to the funeral.

'No, still throwing up daily. But I wanted to talk to you about something.'

'Oh yes?'

'I might as well come out with it.'

'What?' Kaisa sighed. Since Peter had gone, she had no patience for anything. 'C'mon what is it?'

'Come home to Finland!'

'You've been speaking with mum.'

'You know she isn't usually right about much, but this time she has a point. You know the best place to give birth is here in Finland. Helsinki has a fantastic new maternity ward, really close to where mum lives. All you'd need to do is to come over a month before you're due, and stay six weeks after the birth. If you want to go back to London, well then you could. Just for the duration of your maternity leave. I'm sure the BBC would let you go earlier under the circumstances.'

Kaisa didn't reply. She wondered if Sirkka might be right. How lovely it would be to be looked after by your own family. To let Sirkka and Pirjo make the decisions for her, and to be in a familiar place when the baby was born. That would be wonderful, wouldn't it?

Sirkka continued, 'Just think, the cousins would get to know you, and you could come over for long visits to Rovaniemi. We could go for a walk with the babies in their prams! How fantastic it would be to have so much time together.'

'OK, I'll think about it.' Kaisa thought there was nothing stopping her from going to see her sister in Lapland whether she was in London or Helsinki, but she let it drop. She didn't want the same argument with Sirkka as she had had with her mother.

'That's wonderful!'

'I said, I'd think about it, not that I'd do it!'

'OK! How are you feeling anyway?'

Kaisa told Sirkka about the end of the hormone injections and how she was actually feeling pretty good. Poor Sirkka had been very sick from almost the beginning. The sisters exchanged a few more pregnancy stories, before Kaisa said she had to go. Ravi had made a mild curry and was gesticulating from the kitchen to say the food was ready.

Over supper, Kaisa told Ravi how tempting it would be to just go back to Finland.

'I can't rely on you forever,' she said and looked down at her plate.

Ravi put his hand over Kaisa's and she was struck how pale her skin looked against Ravi's mocha shade. 'I want to help.' His eyes were gazing directly at Kaisa. 'So no more nonsense about my generosity. You're like a sister to me, Kaisa. I don't know what I'd do without you.'

Kaisa could feel tears welling up inside her, but she held them back and smiled at Ravi instead. 'That's decided then.

I want the little one to be born in England, however much less fabulous and world class the facilities!'

'That's my girl.'

THAT NIGHT, waking after just a few hours sleep, Kaisa thought about her conversation with Ravi and about her sister's words. Would she be better off moving back to Finland after all? She knew she might be able to get a job with the national broadcaster, YLE, or possibly with one of the commercial radio stations that had sprung up all over Finland. They were relaying programmes that Kaisa and the other reporters at the BBC were producing, so she would be known to the management teams in these companies.

The thought of being at home again, with family around her, was very appealing. Especially if she could find work and a place to live. But the thought of leaving the Notting Hill house that she had shared with Peter was unthinkable. There were so many memories here: the white, impractical sofa they'd bought together; the bench in the hall; the wobbly kitchen table that Peter had found in the second-hand shop on Portobello Road; and the pictures on the walls bought during their trips to France with Ravi.

The house itself seemed to breathe Peter. She smiled when she recalled the day they moved in, how they'd vowed to make love in each room, and how they had. They'd even made love in the kitchen, where on one afternoon in the middle of a London heatwave, Peter had entered Kaisa from behind, while she leaned onto the wobbly kitchen table. Kaisa remembered how much they had wanted each other. No, this house held too many wonderful memories. Kaisa couldn't leave this place, or this country. Britain was – had been – Peter's home, and it would be the home of his child too.

The next morning when Kaisa woke after another restless night, there was a letter on the mat. She recognised the writing immediately, and tore open the envelope.

'Dear Kaisa,

    I hope you are coping, but I know it must be hard. I have been speaking with your mother ...'

KAISA PUT her hand to her mouth. Her father had been speaking with her mother! She walked into the kitchen, flicked the kettle on and continued reading.

'We both agree that you should come back home. Unlike your mother, I don't interfere in the lives of my grown-up daughters, but on this occasion I must give you my opinion. You are expecting a child.

    As your father, I know that having a baby when there are two parents isn't easy. To do it on your own is very difficult indeed. And you are planning to have this baby on your own in a foreign country.

    You know I very much respected Peter and know he was a good husband and would have made a good father. But, it is not to be. So you need your family around you.

    Come home to Finland, this is isänmaasi.

    Greetings, Dad.'

Kaisa sat down at the kitchen table and stared at the words. She tried to think when – if ever – she'd had a letter from her father. And he had used that word, *isänmaa,* fatherland, which he must have known would bring a lump to her throat.

'Bad news?' Ravi stood in the doorway, with a concerned look on his face. He was wearing a thick, dark green Prince of Wales checked dressing gown and his smart black leather slippers.

Kaisa translated the letter for Ravi, fighting tears, while Ravi picked up a mug from the wooden tree next to the kettle and made himself tea. He then measured coffee into a cafetière and poured the rest of the hot water over the top.

He turned back to face Kaisa. 'It's OK. If you want to go back to Finland, you should.'

Kaisa sighed and closed her eyes. 'I don't know what to do.'

TWENTY-NINE

Kaisa had come to fear the nights since Peter's death. During the initial weeks, she'd fallen into bed in a kind of coma from all the crying, usually forced there by her mother or later by Ravi, who would make her a cup of soothing camomile tea and sit by the bed until she fell asleep (or pretended to).

Thinking about the baby usually made her settle, but she'd be awake again a few hours later, in the dead of night, at first blissfully unaware of Peter's death. When reality hit her, she would feel as though someone had punched her in the stomach. She'd feel winded and close to being sick. To calm herself she'd often place her hand on her growing belly and try to think about what Mrs D, her therapist, had told her.

'Try to be grateful and think about what Peter gave you during his life.'

After Kaisa's mother had left, Ravi had got Kaisa in touch with the analyst. 'Just go and see her once,' he'd said. 'For me.'

Kaisa had promised and had immediately liked the grey-haired woman with wise, kind brown eyes. Mrs D, whose second name, she said, was 'unpronounceable', saw her 'clients' as she called the people who came to her home in smart Holland Park.

Kaisa sat opposite Mrs D in a small room while they talked about Kaisa's feelings. For the first sessions, Kaisa spoke less than Mrs D, fearing she'd embarrass herself with an inconsolable crying fit, or even rage, as she'd done when her mother had been staying with her.

Gradually, however, she managed to talk about Peter without tears. She told Mrs D how they had met under the sparkling chandeliers of the British Embassy in Helsinki, about her engagement to the Finnish Matti, about his death, about Kaisa's difficulties in getting used to life as a Navy Wife in Britain, and about the short separation from Peter.

Finally, she told her about her miscarriages and how happy Peter had been during that last phone call home, when he'd found out she was pregnant and receiving treatment that would ensure the baby's survival.

'You must be so glad that he knew about the baby,' Mrs D said to Kaisa on her fourth or fifth visit, and Kaisa, looking up at the wise grey eyes of the older woman, nodded.

'You were lucky.'

'Lucky?' Kaisa replied, her mouth open in amazement.

'Many of the bereaved people I see didn't get the chance to share good news or express their love, like you and Peter did, before their partner is taken away.'

Kaisa looked at her hands resting below her round belly. The baby inside her now kicked properly. When this happened, she'd feel tears prick her eyelids at the thought that she wasn't able to tell Peter about it. She hadn't once considered herself lucky (*lucky!*) for being able to tell Peter she was pregnant again, or for being able to say she loved him. Those words, *You've made me the happiest man alive*, now rang in Kaisa's ears and she saw she was indeed fortunate.

AFTER SHE'D BEEN SEEING Mrs D for a few weeks, Kaisa began to sleep better. At the same time, she started to have vivid dreams about making love to Peter. Waking after such a dream, she'd feel so happy at the prospect of his homecoming, until she remembered that he would never again walk along the front garden and hurriedly take her into his arms, while closing the front door with his foot.

Sometimes Kaisa would dream she was kissing him at a cocktail party onboard a ship, in full view of everybody. He'd grab her behind, just as he had when they'd first met at the British Embassy in Helsinki all those years ago. He had been slightly drunk that evening, having already represented Britain at three other embassies. On the dance floor, in front of the Finnish Foreign Minister and his wife, a former model, Peter had squeezed her bottom. But unlike on that first wonderful evening with her beloved Englishman, when Kaisa had removed his hand and told him off, in the dream, Kaisa ignored the gasps of the other wives and honoured guests.

Once she dreamed that Lady Di came to speak to her at such a party and told her that if she'd been married to Peter she would never let him out of her sight. After that dream Kaisa woke with an intense feeling of jealousy, until she remembered that Peter was no longer alive. She then felt queasy, as if a heavy plate had been placed on her chest and she couldn't breathe. After she'd calmed herself down, she put the light on and pulled a letter out from a pile in her bedside drawer. She lost count of how many notes she'd received from people who had known Peter. Some of the messages were short, some beautifully written with the same kind of old-fashioned fountain pen that Peter had used. But one letter was more special than the others. The sheet of heavy yellow paper had a beautiful crest made out of her initial, with a crown perching on top of the 'D' above the text 'Kensington Palace'. It had arrived a few days after Peter's death, but Kaisa hadn't read any of the notes until weeks later.

> *Dear Kesa,*
>
> *I was so distressed to hear that your husband, Lieutenant Commander Peter Williams, who I had the pleasure to meet onboard HMS Redoubt in May this year, perished during an accident. I remember him as a very polite and charming naval officer and can only imagine what sorrow his passing has caused you and your family.*
>
> *Please accept my warmest condolences.*
>
> *Yours sincerely,*
>
> *Diana*

THE LETTER WAS TYPED, but the Princess had hand-written the greeting and signed it. She'd misspelled Kaisa's name, but Kaisa knew it was probably a mistake by one of her courtiers, or whatever the people working for her were called. The words alone were lovely, as was the personal touch. She guessed that correspondence from the Princess had caused that particular succession of images in her dream.

Kaisa placed the heavy sheet of paper back in its envelope and put the letter on top of the others in her bedside drawer and climbed back into bed. She tried to rekindle the dream, just to feel Peter's hands on her and his breath close to her skin again.

THIRTY

K aisa was lying on her bed, waiting for Rosa to wake up. It was nearly six am, and she knew it would be a matter of minutes before she heard her daughter call out for her. It wasn't quite light yet, but Kaisa hadn't slept well, and around five am had given up and begun reading a new book that Ravi had given her, *A Secret History* by Donna Tart. Ravi had become Kaisa's new supplier of fiction, as well as her best friend, an excellent cook and her private fashion adviser. Kaisa would be starving and in rags if it wasn't for Ravi. She sighed. She'd miss him dreadfully.

She was so grateful for everything he had done for her; especially now she knew about his secret. She worried for him, because after the accident, he had been with her night and day, and he didn't seem to have a steady boyfriend. She'd wanted to ask him if he had casual relationships and to urge him to be careful, but each time she approached the matter, even in a roundabout way, he'd change the subject.

Once, when they'd been sitting at the kitchen table, a few days after Rosa's birth, and the radio was playing

'These are the days of our lives' by Queen, Kaisa had been brave enough to speak honestly with him. Ravi had been holding Kaisa's hands between his, and Kaisa had looked at the few dark hairs growing between the knuckles on the back of his fingers, fighting the memory of Peter's beautiful long fingers, which had hairs growing on them in exactly the same way. Ravi's skin was a shade darker, and his fingernails looked almost feminine in their paleness and cleanliness. Kaisa looked up at Ravi's dark brown eyes and said, 'Ravi, you are being careful, aren't you?'

The death of Freddie Mercury the year before had brought back the memory of Duncan struggling to breathe as he lay in the iron bed in Dorset.

'I couldn't bear to lose another ...'

Ravi had straightened up and looked startled. 'Of course.' He dropped Kaisa's hands and ran one of his own hands through his black, shiny hair. He'd grown it longer, Kaisa now saw, and wondered if it was because he didn't have time to go to the barbers anymore. She knew he didn't want to leave her at home in the afternoons, so each day he hurried back from his job in the City.

'Ravi, I'm just worried about you,' Kaisa had added.

'Oh Kaisa,' he'd said and leaned back on the ancient pine chair, which creaked slightly under his weight. 'I can't talk about it.'

Kaisa had hugged Ravi, and at that moment they'd both heard Rosa stirring. She got up and said, 'Just promise you're careful?'

Ravi had looked down at the table and nodded.

'I promise.'

KAISA WAS FEEDING Rosa her morning porridge in the

kitchen when she heard the doorbell go. She looked at her watch; it was only just gone eight so this had to be Peter's parents. She wiped the little girl's mouth, marvelled at her beautiful dark green eyes, which were the exact shape and shade of Peter's, and lifted her up.

'Shall we go and say hello to Granny and Grandpa?'

Rosa giggled and said, 'Ganny, Ganny!'

The girl, who looked almost nothing like Kaisa, having inherited the dark hair and eyes of the Williams family, loved her 'Ganny'. Peter's mother, Evelyn, or 'Evie' as everyone called her, had turned out to be a real rock; after the accident, she and Peter's father had rushed up to London from their home in Wiltshire.

Kaisa had never been very close to Evie, mainly because of the events in Scotland, which had caused so much heartache for her son, not to mention the harm it had done to Peter's career. Kaisa fully understood how she felt; if it had been her, she too would have been sceptical about a daughter-in-law who cheated on her husband after only six months of marriage.

But since the terrible accident, Peter's mum had been an angel, visiting Kaisa often after her own mother had gone back to Finland, initially shedding tears with her, sharing her grief, which, after all, to her, must have been even worse. Now a mother herself, Kaisa could only imagine how much Evie suffered from losing a child.

Kaisa didn't want to think about what she had to tell them later that day.

When Rosa was born, Evie, together with her own mother, were once again at Kaisa's side, holding her hand as Kaisa cried and screamed her way through the labour. Now Evie popped up to London once of twice a month, babysitting for Kaisa as often as she could, and saving on Rosa's nursery costs.

Sometimes when Kaisa was saying goodbye to Rosa, as Peter's mother held the little girl on her lap, singing nursery rhymes to soften the blow of her mother's departure, she wondered if there was criticism in Evie's voice when she told Rosa, 'Mummy has to go to work, darling, doesn't she?'

She'd often have a look in her pale eyes, a look that said, 'How can you leave this little girl, a gift you were so desperate to have, and all you have left of Peter?' But true to her English manners, she never voiced those criticisms and Kaisa was too tired and too afraid to hear the truth to begin a discussion on the matter. And perhaps she was imagining such criticism.

Kaisa knew she didn't have to go to work, because of the generous pension she was getting from the Navy. Lieutenant Commander Crowther, who still wrote to her and even telephoned to ask how she was, and if there was anything he could do for her, had organised all the paperwork regarding the pension and the death certificate. He had also put Peter's affairs in order, including the mortgage, which was paid off with a life policy. He had communicated all the details to Ravi. A month or so after the funeral, Ravi had sat Kaisa down and told her that she was quite a wealthy woman.

'Peter certainly made sure you would be alright, and the Navy are being very generous.'

Kaisa had nodded. *What was money compared to having Peter alive and with her?* But she had thanked Ravi and thought about what Mrs D kept telling her: *Think of the positives.* Peter had loved her and had made sure she would not have to worry about money if he died before her.

She knew she was being selfish for staying at the BBC,

but she needed time away from her home life and the dreadful longing she had for Peter. Sitting at home alone with Rosa, she would, she was sure, obsess about Peter. She wanted to see him just once more; to hear his voice; to feel his lips on her; and his body pressed against hers. She needed an escape from that longing, even if it lasted only as long as her news broadcasts on John Major's new, flailing government, or the IRA terror attacks in London and elsewhere.

It was her job at the BBC that had saved her from going crazy after Peter's funeral. She knew the only way she'd keep herself sane was to get back to the work she loved, the only place that hadn't changed.

THIRTY-ONE

I t was a sunny day on the second anniversary of Peter's death. As if to mock her grief, there wasn't a cloud in the sky. Her psychiatrist said she needed to 'let go of her guilt'.

During the sessions she'd taken with the grey-haired analyst, Kaisa had learned more about herself than she thought possible. How she blamed herself for Peter's accident; how she couldn't accept that it was just a random event with disastrous consequences; how she fretted about having no control over it.

Although Kaisa now saw Mrs D only every two months, she had insisted on weekly sessions during the month before the anniversary. Before making Kaisa do the customary relaxation exercises, she'd reminded Kaisa that the only thing she could control was how she spent the rest of her life. Did she want to find the negative, and be sad on the second anniversary of Peter's death, or did she, for her own sake as much as for her daughter's and Peter's family's sake, want to celebrate her late husband's life? Did she want to feel grateful for the love she had shared with Peter and the love she now had for her daughter and her family and friends?

Kaisa had cried and wanted to mourn. She wanted to be sad, she wanted to cry until it was all over, and Peter walked through the door of their little house again, carrying his Pusser's Grip, smiling at her before he bent down and kissed her lips.

She wanted to howl at the unfairness of it all. She wanted to scream and shout at Mrs D, tell her how unfair it was that her memory of Peter's kisses was fading. If only she'd had the chance to take more pictures of him, to record the sound of his voice. All she had was the wedding video made by her uncle, which didn't include Peter's voice. But deep inside, she knew Mrs D was right; she couldn't let Rosa grow up in a home that was sad, and she needed to consider Peter's family too.

PETER'S PARENTS drove Kaisa to Kensal Green cemetery in their new Ford Mondeo. Kaisa still had Peter's old Golf GTi, but if it was a sunny day she'd often visit Peter's grave by walking to Westbourne Park Tube station and taking the number 18 bus from there, pushing Rosa in her pram when she was a baby and later in her buggy.

She still hated driving in London, even though she'd done it for years. The traffic around Notting Hill seemed only to get worse and finding a space to park near her home was becoming more and more difficult.

As she fixed Rosa into her car seat, and watched her kick her feet in excitement at being with her grandparents, 'Gampi' and 'Ganny', she resolved that she would heed Mrs D's advice and celebrate Peter's life rather than mourn him today. But she was also worried about how Peter's parents would react to her news. Kaisa decided not to think about that now; she'd tell them later when there was a quiet moment before the guests arrived. She knew she was putting it off, but she needed Ravi's support when she told them what she knew would be a great blow to them.

'Alright?' Evie said from the front seat, turning around to smile at Kaisa and Rosa.

Kaisa nodded quickly, feeling caught out by the older woman's straight gaze. Rosa kicked and waved her hands, pulling her body towards her granny, so that her seatbelt cut into her tummy.

'We'll soon be there, lovey,' Evie cooed and stroked the little girl's stubby fingers.

Kaisa gave her daughter a stick of carrot to suck at. She was teething and would chew at anything Kaisa gave her. 'Ready to go,' she said, and Peter's father started the engine.

ONCE THE FOUR of them were out of the car, and walking underneath the tall arches of the cemetery entrance, Kaisa felt a longing so severe in the pit of her stomach that she had to gasp. Evie was next to her, with one hand resting on Rosa's buggy. She put her other hand behind Kaisa's back, supporting her during their walk towards Peter's grave. Kaisa gave her mother-in-law a grateful smile. She pointed at a flower stall set up to the left of the chapel where they had attended the short ceremony two years ago.

'Let's get some flowers,' Evie said.

Kaisa nodded, unable to speak.

Although she came here almost every week, and always made the same purchase of a single red rose to put on Peter's grave, today the ritual felt more poignant, more final. She felt tears well behind her eyelids when she remembered the very first time Peter had given her a red rose at Helsinki airport, just before he boarded a plane to London.

Kaisa had cried all the way home on the bus, desolate that she had to say goodbye to her beloved Englishman. How she wished she'd understood that those were the happy times. How lucky she had been then! To be able to look forward to seeing Peter again, to be able to count the weeks and days until she could feel his lips on hers, his body pressed against hers.

Now the counting was backwards; how long since their last conversation on the telephone, how many days, weeks, months and years since they'd made love, how long since she'd seen his smile, or smelled his familiar scent of coconut aftershave and something else, something musky and manly.

She needed to remember all these things, and yet she was afraid that little by little she was forgetting them. She had the photographs of him smiling next to his yellow, open-top Spitfire, another one in which he is dressed up for a wedding, from the time before she knew him. There were pictures from their own wedding in Finland, and the first hastily arranged registry office ceremony in Portsmouth. There were a few photographs of Peter and Kaisa together on various submarines and ships, at parties and naval dances, holding each other close, smiling into the camera.

Kaisa often examined her own face, as well as that of Peter, and wondered who that smiling woman was, and how Peter felt about her. She regretted each row they'd had, and they had had many. Too many.

She couldn't comprehend how she had been so stupid to sleep with another man, and then foolish enough to leave Peter alone in Scotland, a decision that had parted them for nearly a year. Her head had been full of feminist rhetoric, of pacifism, and opposition to the Navy. The Royal Navy that had been Peter's first love. How remote those beliefs now seemed! But Kaisa knew – as Mrs D had helped her remember – that they'd also had many happy times, as witnessed by the smiling couple in those pictures.

Yet she didn't recognise herself in those photographs; in spite of all the sessions with Mrs D, she had to work hard to find joy in life since Peter's death. If it hadn't been for the pregnancy, and for Rosa, this wonderful, beautiful girl – Peter's daughter – Kaisa didn't know what would have happened to her. She sighed and paid the florist for her rose.

'Here you are, Mrs Williams,' the woman said kindly. She had messy grey hair, which was trying to escape from a stripey scarf tied around her head. She knew Kaisa, and knew what she would order. 'Special day today, is it?' she said, nodding with a smile at Peter's mother and father, who, holding onto the handlebar of Rosa's buggy, were standing a little further away, looking at the buckets of flowers on the other side of the stall.

'Two years today,' Kaisa managed to say.

'I'm so sorry,' the woman said, and then lifting her brown eyes at Kaisa, added, 'It gets better, my dear.'

'Thank you,' Kaisa said and turned away. Kindness, or kind words, were almost the worst, she'd found. Although it was better than the silence many people offered when they heard about what had happened to Peter. It was strange to her how many people were afraid of the word 'death' and preferred talking about 'passing away' or 'loss', as if by simply being careless, Kaisa had let Peter slip away.

Now, two years later, Kaisa had learned to fight the images of the accident running through her head, how Peter must have fought to try and get breath as his body was pulled under the dark waves. After Lieutenant Commander Crowther, or Stephen, had told her the gruesome details, she'd tried to ask Nigel, who, after all, had been there, how Peter had fallen into the water. It was during a phone call months afterwards, but Nigel had only said, 'He slipped up.' His wife, Kaisa's friend Pammy, had told her of Nigel's breakdown after Peter's death. Neither of them had been able to come to the funeral. Nigel had been on strong medication for six months and was now on permanent sick leave from the Navy.

AT THE GRAVESIDE, or at the memorial stone as it was correctly called, since what was left of Peter had been cremated and wasn't in the ground, Kaisa remembered how she hadn't been able to take any tranquillisers after the accident, due to the baby. She had been almost jealous of the oblivion Nigel's drugs had given him. Pammy had told her over the telephone that he seemed to do nothing but sleep at the unit he'd been taken to. For weeks he hadn't even recognised Pammy or their two daughters.

'Gampi is going to say a few words,' Evie said, now at her side, bringing Kaisa back to the present day.

She nodded and saw that Rosa was sitting still in her buggy for once, staring at the small patch of grass where Peter's mother had placed the pot of bright red geraniums she'd bought, next to Kaisa's red rose, which she had placed in the vase she'd bought a few weeks after the funeral.

THE GREEN, plastic vial stood in front of the stone, with the inscription:

Peter, My Beloved,
Our Dearest Son
Brother and Uncle
We Love You Always
Born 10 April 1960
Died 30 September 1990

THIRTY-TWO

Ravi was already standing by the door when Peter's father double parked in front of the house to drop everyone off. Kaisa removed the sleeping Rosa from the car seat and Peter's mum went to get the buggy out of the back. Evie suffered from back pain, but the older woman straightened herself up and said, 'I'm fine.' Kaisa smiled. Evie wanted to be useful.

'I'm early,' Ravi said, walking up to the car. He still held keys to the house and had obviously let himself in. He kissed Kaisa on the cheek.

Peter's father wasn't used to parking in small spaces, so Ravi got into the driver's seat and smartly manoeuvred the Ford into a space a little way along the road.

'Thank you very much, young man,' Peter's father said when Ravi handed him back the keys.

Kaisa smiled, theirs was an unusual friendship. From what she knew of Peter's parents they were not exactly racist, but at the same time they were not used to seeing anything other than white faces where they lived. The only immigrants were the Free Polish who'd come over during and immediately after the Second World War.

'Brave people, brave people,' Kaisa had heard Peter's dad say about the Poles in their town.

Apart from the race issue, Kaisa also knew her friendship with Ravi could be misconstrued, especially as she knew Peter's parents had no idea about Ravi's sexuality. However, both parents seemed to be grateful to Ravi for all the time he spent looking after Kaisa and Rosa.

It was amazing how a death and a birth brought people together, Kaisa thought, as she watched Peter's father and Ravi walk side by side along the front path to the house. The men's heads were bent over in conversation, and Peter's dad had his hand on Ravi's shoulder. His white head against Ravi's jet-black hair and darker skin made the pair look positively exotic.

'Alright?' Kaisa heard Peter's mum ask behind her. Ravi had managed to wrangle the heavy buggy out of the older woman's hands, before he'd helped to park the car, and she was now standing behind Kaisa on the narrow path. Kaisa realised Peter's mother was cold; she had her arms crossed and was rubbing her arms with her hands.

'Yes, sorry, miles away,' Kaisa said and moved towards the house, carrying Rosa.

Ravi came up to her. He smelled of his usual orange-scented aftershave. When he bent down to give the sleeping Rosa a peck on her forehead, the girl squirmed in Kaisa's arms.

'I'm going to take her up for her nap. We might then get an hour or so to have lunch. Anyone else arrived yet?' she asked Ravi.

'No,' Ravi shook his head. 'I can take her up,' he added, giving Kaisa a look, which said, 'Here's your chance.'

Kaisa shook her head. She went up the stairs and settled the sleeping child into her cot. For a while she sat on her bed; she needed to steel herself. She looked at her watch, there was still time to speak with Peter's parents before her guests arrived.

She put her hand on Rosa's tummy. She'd decided to keep the cot in her bedroom even though there was a smaller bedroom at the back of the house, which she and Peter had thought might become a nursery one day. Ravi had been using it as his bedroom and an unofficial office when he had papers to read for work, and Kaisa wasn't in any hurry to move Rosa away from her bedroom.

Kaisa gazed at the sleeping child. She'd covered Rosa's legs with her favourite pink blanket, which Evie had crocheted for her. Sleepily, the child had grabbed a corner with one hand and was now holding onto it with her chubby fingers. She was so beautiful, with her dark curls mussed around her head on the pillow and her long black eyelashes resting on her pale round cheekbones. Her little mouth was pale pink, with the arch of her lips perfectly drawn. For a moment, the thought that Peter would never see how beautiful she was hit her with such force that her chest felt as if it had collapsed and she struggled to breathe. *Think of the positives, think of the positives*, she repeated in her head, and she concentrated on taking in air through her nose and blowing it out of her mouth as Mrs D had taught her.

'Celebrate his life, instead of mourning his death. And don't worry about upsetting others. This is your life to lead the way you decide is best for you and Rosa,' she'd said as Kaisa had left her office.

When Kaisa's breathing had returned to normal, she gave her daughter a last glance, made sure the baby alarm on the bedside table had its green lights on, and returned downstairs.

ALL THE GUESTS arrived at the same time; Rose and Roger had driven up from Dorset, Peter's best man Jeff and his wife, Milly, from Portsmouth, Nigel and Pammy from Plymouth and even Stephen had made it. Kaisa knew he was now working up in Whitehall, and they'd met a few times at the Army Navy Club in St James's, but he still lived up in Scotland.

Peter's brother Simon had grown very grey during the last year. His wife Miriam gave Kaisa a present for Rosa.

'Thank you, that's very kind of you,' Kaisa said.

'Even though she doesn't understand, I'm sure she'll find this day difficult, so here's something to take her mind off it,' Miriam said, giving Kaisa a short, efficient hug.

Peter's sister Nancy had brought her twins, but said she was sorry her husband couldn't make it. The boy and girl, Oliver and Beth, who had just turned seven, ran in and out through the French doors, in a game no one understood.

Kaisa thought how lucky they were to have a sunny day. She was also not sorry, if she was truthful, that Nancy's loud husband hadn't come. He had the knack of saying the wrong thing, and she knew Peter hadn't much cared for him. The twins were wild, but no one minded. It was good to have children around. They were oblivious to the sadness of the occasion, and happily munched on sandwiches while running around the adults. Kaisa thought how strikingly similar they looked to Peter, and to Rosa, with their mops of dark hair, pale skin and long, lean bodies. Rosa, however, was still chubby, although her long legs and arms hinted at a lankiness to come.

Rose hugged Kaisa hard; and Kaisa held onto her friend for a bit longer than was safe. Too much kindness was still a problem, and could set her off crying at any moment, but she held it together, reminding herself that she needed to be grateful for what she had: the love of Peter's family, her friends and her lovely daughter Rosa.

Rose, after whom Kaisa had partly named her daughter, had also been a great support to Kaisa after Peter's death. She'd been to stay with Kaisa a few times, and had co-ordinated her visit with Ravi, so that it coincided with a work trip Ravi had to take to the States. The two of them had laughed and cried, remembering all the crazy days at the feminist magazine, *Adam's Apple*.

'Without you, I'm not sure Peter and I would have ever got back together,' Kaisa once said during such a conversation.

Rose had looked down at her hands, then lifted her eyes to Kaisa and remarked, 'I'm not sure without my family's interference you would have ever separated.'

Duncan's passing hadn't been mentioned by either Rose or Kaisa, nor Ravi. It was as if Rose didn't want to lump the two men together and Kaisa was grateful for her friend's tactfulness.

The memory of Duncan, of the one stupid drunken night, of the AIDS scare it had led to, and his sad, sad death, made Kaisa want to howl with anger and frustration with herself. Rose had put her arms around Kaisa and rocked her back and forth. 'I'm sorry, darling, I don't mean to upset you.'

'You look well,' Rose now said, eventually letting go of Kaisa.

'So do you!' Suddenly Kaisa noticed that Rose was wearing a loose, sky-blue dress. She looked at her tummy, then at her eyes, which looked bluish, reflecting the bright colour of the dress.

'You're not?'

A wide smile brightened Rose's face, 'It's early days yet.'

'Congratulations!' Kaisa gave her friend another hug.

'I'm over forty, so I know I'm too old, but apparently I'm as healthy as a horse.' Rose turned to her husband, who also had a wide smile on his face. Kaisa shook Roger's hand and gave him a kiss on the cheek. 'I'm so very, very happy for you both.'

Kaisa had spoken with Pammy and Nigel on the phone several times, but this was the first time since Peter's death that the two friends had seen each other.

When they arrived at the door, Kaisa was shocked to see how frail Nigel looked; he'd lost a lot of weight and didn't look at all well. His eyes looked watery and sad, and for a moment Kaisa thought he'd cry when he hugged Kaisa without being able to speak.

Right after the funeral, when Pammy had phoned and apologised for not coming, and told Kaisa about Nigel's breakdown, Kaisa had wanted to apologise to Nigel, and Pammy. She felt responsible for his grief. Peter's death had nothing to do with Nigel, she knew that.

When Kaisa saw Jeff, she had to fight tears once more. Peter's best friend had been such a support to her in the early days of their marriage when they still lived in Portsmouth. Kaisa had often wondered whether, if they'd stayed in Southsea instead of moving up to Scotland, she would have been happier and, with Jeff's friendship, been able to resist Duncan.

Jeff had put on a little weight, and was beginning to resemble his father, one of the witnesses at Peter and Kaisa's hastily arranged registry office wedding all those years ago.

When Jeff enveloped Kaisa in his arms, just like the bear hug his father usually gave her, Kaisa felt a little guilty for not inviting Jeff's parents. They'd made the journey up from Portsmouth on the day of Peter's funeral two years ago, and she'd been surprised to see them then. But today, she'd decided on just her and Peter's closest friends and family.

Looking at the now crowded room, she wondered how everyone had fitted in on the day of the funeral. The memory of that day was so hazy. She remembered spending some of it sitting alone in the kitchen, being unsociable and not caring if she was.

'You OK, darling?' Jeff asked, letting go of Kaisa and rubbing her back with his hand.

'Yes, I'm good,' Kaisa replied and turned to Milly, Jeff's wife. She too had got a bit rounder in the middle. She was wearing a loose navy dress, with a single string of pearls around her neck and a pair of flat suede pumps on her feet.

'You didn't bring the girls?' Kaisa asked. Milly had given birth to two children in quick succession after the wedding. Peter had said that she was 'up the duff' already, before they got married. Their first daughter, Catherine, had been born only five months afterwards.

'God no, they're with their grandparents,' Milly said and gave a short laugh.

Kaisa had never really got to know Milly. When Jeff had met her and married very quickly, Peter and Kaisa had been separated, and after they got back together again and settled in London, there hadn't been many opportunities to meet up with Peter's old friend and his new wife. Kaisa now wondered if Milly didn't like her because of what she had done to Peter and this was why there had been no invitations to visit Portsmouth. Mind you, Peter and Kaisa had also not asked them to visit London. Weekends together had seemed so precious that Kaisa rarely wanted to share them with anyone.

A stab of longing suddenly took hold of Kaisa and she forced herself to think of the good times, just as Mrs D had told her. She smiled at Milly, 'How old are they now?'

'Oh,' Milly regarded Kaisa critically. Had she noticed Kaisa's fake smile and interpreted it wrongly?

'Cath is six and Poppy five. Complete nightmare ages – can't wait to ship them off to boarding school,' Milly said turning her face towards Jeff.

Kaisa nodded. She looked to the side and saw Rose, standing on her own by the French doors. She raised her eyebrows at Kaisa, who returned the look with a smile. She turned to Ravi, who'd appeared beside her, 'You've met Peter's friends Jeff and Milly, haven't you?'

'Yes, two years ago,' Ravi said carefully, and shook their hands. He asked what they wanted to drink and Kaisa excused herself and moved towards Rose.

'You OK?' Rose said, leaning against the doorframe of the French windows.

'I'm just about to tell everyone the news.'

Rose nodded. Kaisa had phoned her friend as soon as she'd made her decision and although Rose had been quiet at the end of the phone, she'd admitted that she knew why Kaisa was doing what she was planning. She looked at Rose's kind face and said, 'Would you stay here for a bit of moral support?'

'Of course,' Rose said, and placed her hand on Kaisa's arm. 'I'm here for you. Always.'

With Rose by her side, Kaisa got an empty glass and gave it a tap with a spoon. She wanted everyone present for her announcement, but now that it came to it, she felt nervous.

Suddenly the low chatter that had accompanied the sound of cutlery against the white china plates, stopped and all the faces in the room looked up at Kaisa. She swallowed. It was going to be hard to deliver her news. She glanced at Peter's mother, who had looked pale and serious since she'd spoken to her and Peter's father in the lounge that morning. Evie now seemed to have tears in her eyes. It had been terrible to tell them, and Kaisa had been glad of Ravi's presence. She knew it wasn't easy for him, especially when Peter's mother had blurted out, 'I thought you two were going to get married and that was what this was all about.'

Ravi had looked at his hands, not able to face Kaisa, it seemed, nor the couple opposite.

Kaisa had felt anger towards Peter's parents at that point. She knew Ravi wasn't ashamed of being gay, but at the same time she knew he wouldn't want Peter's parents to know, because it had nothing to do with them. Still, Kaisa felt the unfairness of it all acutely. Why would Peter's parents assume that everyone was the same? But Kaisa had kept her voice steady when she'd said, 'Actually I only made the decision after I'd invited you all to celebrate Peter's life on the second anniversary. I thought it very important we commemorate it every year.'

'Of course,' Evie had replied.

Now she moved her eyes away from Kaisa, and put her hand through the crook of her husband's arm. His eyes were steady on Kaisa, but she couldn't help seeing a hardness in them. Was he also angry with Kaisa for wanting a new life for her and Rosa?

'I wanted to thank you all for coming today. Especially Peter's parents, for whom I know this day is a difficult one. I'd also like to thank, you, Ravi, for being my rock, and Rose,' Kaisa's mouth felt parched and she smiled at her friend, but turning back to the room carried on, 'All of you who are dear friends: Jeff, Milly, Pammy and Nigel. And thank you Stephen for all your help,' Kaisa nodded to the tall man in the corner of the room who she'd convinced to come to the lunch. 'Peter's brother and sister and Miriam. I am very grateful to all of you for your support over the past two years. I hope you know that.'

Kaisa glanced around the room, meeting the eyes of the people she'd thanked. Her gaze came to rest on Ravi. His brown eyes looked even more like liquid than usual. Kaisa knew he was unhappy about her decision. There was a general murmur around the room and the twins, Oliver and Ruth clapped their hands. Everyone laughed.

Kaisa cleared her throat. She wasn't finished yet. 'I also wanted to let you know that after having thought about this long and hard ever since ...' Kaisa swallowed again, her mouth feeling too dry to carry on. 'Excuse me for a moment,' she said and reached for a glass of water.

'What I wanted to tell you is that I am moving back to Finland.'

THIRTY-THREE

A week before she was due to move, amidst all the packing, Kaisa met Rose to say goodbye. She'd taken a cab to make it easier to get to Terroni's with Rosa and her buggy. As she stepped out, she was met by Toni outside the café, and soon the little girl was in Toni's arms and being taken into the café to be fussed over by the whole Terroni family.

'Bella, bella, Rosa!' Mamma said and fed the little girl tiny pieces of pink Italian meringue.

Rose was already sitting at 'their table' in the corner, sipping herbal tea.

'You've gone off coffee, then?' Kaisa asked.

Rose nodded, and Kaisa looked at Rosa sitting on top of the counter, held by Mamma. 'She'd be a little fat girl if I stayed here, with Toni and his family feeding her all the wrong things!'

Toni was convinced Kaisa had given her daughter an Italian name, however much she tried to explain that Rosa was also common in Finland.

Both Rose and Kaisa laughed. Then, after Toni had brought Kaisa a cup of coffee, the two women were quiet.

'You'll come and visit, won't you?'

Rose touched her tummy and said, 'Yes, once this one is out and ready to face travelling.'

Kaisa looked at her friend. She had so much to be grateful for, and she knew she would miss her dreadfully.

'You know I have to do this, right?' she said and Rose, not looking at Kaisa, nodded.

Kaisa took Rose's hands into hers and said, 'Don't be sad. I promise to write often and phone too. And I will come and visit you as soon as the baby is born. Just try to stop me!'

Kaisa told her friend about the large house she was buying in Lauttasaari, a few steps away from the sea.

'There's a beach with a children's play area just along the shore, and I can even get a small boat if I want to. I actually have a private jetty!' she said.

Kaisa hadn't believed how much cheaper the houses in Helsinki were compared to London. The place she'd bought was one of the massive villas she'd admired as a teenager, in the area close to where her old school friend Vappu had lived. Never in her wildest dreams would she have imagined she could ever afford such a place.

Rose smiled. 'It sounds idyllic.'

After a succession of hugs from Toni, Mamma and the rest of the family, Rose and Kaisa, with Rosa now fast asleep in the buggy, walked along the Clerkenwell Road. It was a Tuesday afternoon, around four pm, just before the after-work rush. Seeing the pub, The Yorkshire Grey, where Rose had told Kaisa about Duncan barely two years previously, made Kaisa feel so very old and experienced. She placed her hand in the crook of Rose's arm. 'We'll be OK, won't we?'

Rose stopped in the middle of the road and looked at the sleeping child in the buggy and then at Kaisa. 'Of course you will!'

KAISA GLANCED around the empty house. She was holding Rosa's hand, and now pulled the girl up into her arms. She walked slowly up to the French doors and surveyed the perfectly cut lawn. She'd had a specialist company to sort out the garden before she put the house up for sale. She'd never been much of a gardener, and Peter had never had enough time to do anything more than mow the lawn. It had cost her a pretty penny, but the estate agent had said that it was the only 'home improvement', as he'd put it, that she needed to do to get a good price for the little house. The same company had been commissioned to maintain the garden too, and had cut the lawn and weeded the borders, which were now immaculate with evergreen bushes on both sides of the square space.

Kaisa closed and locked the doors, putting the squirming Rosa onto the floor. Rosa had a new doll, given to her as a leaving present by Peter's parents. It had been a painful farewell visit to Wiltshire, although 'Ganny' had told Kaisa she understood she needed to be close to her own family 'since Peter was no longer here'. For Rosa's sake, there had been no tears, and Kaisa was glad of that.

Rosa now stood up and began tottering around the empty living room, making bubbles with her mouth and hugging the doll close to her. Rosa had already been on an airplane several times during her short life, and loved being pampered by the Finnair air hostesses.

'Gone?' she asked, looking at Kaisa with her dark green eyes.

'We are going soon,' she said, and took the little girl's hand. 'Let's just check we haven't forgotten anything.'

Together with Rosa, Kaisa went slowly up the stairs and walked from room to room, all empty now, except the carpets and light fittings with their shades, which she'd agreed to leave behind.

She'd spent so many happy days with her beloved Peter in this house, but Kaisa knew that even if she wasn't here, she would always hold the happy images in her heart. Whatever their love affair and marriage with Peter had been, it had been true.

All the misunderstanding, rows, secrets and infidelities didn't matter. What mattered was that they had deeply and truly loved each other. And that heartfelt love had produced the little, beautiful marvel that Rosa was.

Kaisa carried her daughter down the stairs and as she did so, she heard the horn of a car outside. Ravi was getting out of his brand new BMW.

'Your chariot awaits,' he said and smiled.

WOULD YOU LIKE TO READ MORE?

Why not sign up for the Readers' Group mailing list and get exclusive, unpublished bonus chapters from *The Nordic Heart* series? You will also get a free copy of the first book in the series, *The Young Heart*, a prequel novella to *The English Heart*.

'Wonderfully intimate and honest.' – Pauliina Ståhlberg, Director of The Finnish Institute in London.

Is she too young to fall in love? A standalone read, *The Young Heart* is a prequel to the acclaimed 1980s romance series, *The Nordic Heart*.

Go to www.helenahalme.com to find out more!

DID YOU ENJOY THE TRUE HEART?

Reviews are equally important to readers and authors. So let everyone know by posting a review. Thank you!

Turn the page for more books by Helena Halme

COFFEE AND VODKA

Eeva doesn't want to remember. But now she's forced to return to Finland and confront her past.

'In Stockholm everything is bigger and better.'

When Pappa announces the family is to leave Finland for a new life in Sweden, 11-year-old Eeva is elated. But in Stockholm Mamma finds feminism, Eeva's sister, Anja, pretends to be Swedish and Pappa struggles to adapt.

And one night, Eeva's world falls apart.

Fast forward 30 years. Now teaching Swedish to foreigners,

Eeva travels back to Finland when her beloved grandmother becomes ill. On the overnight ferry, a chance meeting with her married ex-lover, Yri, prompts family secrets to unravel and buried memories to come flooding back.

It's time for Eeva to find out what really happened all those years ago ...

Coffee and Vodka has it all: family drama, mystery, romance and sisterly love.

If you like Nordic Noir, you'll love this rich Nordic family drama by the Finnish author Helena Halme.

'Coffee and Vodka *is a rich story that stays with us....with moments of brilliance.'* – Dr Mimi Thebo, Bath Spa University.

'*Like the television series* The Bridge, Coffee and Vodka *opens our eyes to facets of a Scandinavian culture that most of us would lump together into one. I loved the way the narrative wove together the viewpoint of Eeva the child and her shock at arriving in a new country, with Eeva the sophisticated adult, returning for the first time to the country of her birth, and finding it both familiar and irretrievably strange.'* – Catriona Troth, Triskele Books.

Pick up *Coffee and Vodka* to discover this brilliant, heart-warming Nordic family drama today!

ALSO BY HELENA HALME

The Nordic Heart Romance Series:

The Young Heart (Prequel)

The English Heart (Book 1)

The Faithful Heart (Book 2)

The Good Heart (Book 3)

The True Heart (Book 4)

Coffee and Vodka: A Nordic family drama

The Red King in Helsinki: Lies, Spies and Gymnastics

ABOUT THE AUTHOR

Helena Halme grew up in Tampere, central Finland, and moved to the UK via Stockholm and Helsinki at the age of 22. She is a former BBC journalist and has also worked as a magazine editor, a bookseller and, until recently, ran a Finnish/British cultural association in London.

Since gaining an MA in Creative Writing at Bath Spa University, Helena has published seven fiction titles, including five in *The Nordic Heart* Romance Series.

Helena lives in North London with her ex-Navy husband and an old stubborn terrier, called Jerry. She loves Nordic Noir and sings along to Abba songs when no one is around.

You can read Helena's blog at www.helenahalme.com, where you can also sign up for her *Readers' Group*.

Find Helena Halme online

www.helenahalme.com
hello@helenahalme.com